WAR HORSE

MICHAEL MORPURGO

SCHOLASTIC INC.

New York Toronto London Auckland

Sydney Mexico City New Delhi Hong Kong

FOR LETTICE

MANY PEOPLE HAVE HELPED ME IN THE WRITING OF THIS BOOK.
IN PARTICULAR I WANT TO THANK CLARE AND ROSALIND,
SEBASTIAN AND HORATIO, JIM HINDSON (VETERINARY SURGEON),
ALBERT WEEKS, THE LATE WILFRED ELLIS
AND THE LATE CAPTAIN BUDGETT—
ALL THREE OCTOGENARIANS IN THE PARISH OF IDDESLEIGH

AUTHOR'S NOTE

IN THE OLD SCHOOL THEY USE NOW FOR THE VILLAGE HALL, below the clock that has stood always at one minute past ten, hangs a small dusty painting of a horse. He stands, a splendid red bay with a remarkable white cross emblazoned on his forehead and with four perfectly matched white socks. He looks wistfully out of the picture, his ears pricked forward, his head turned as if he has just noticed us standing there.

To many who glance up at it casually, as they might do when the hall is opened up for parish meetings, for harvest suppers or evening socials, it is merely a tarnished old oil painting of some unknown horse by a competent but anonymous artist. To them the picture is so familiar that it commands little attention. But those who look more closely will see, written in fading black copperplate across the bottom of the bronze frame:

JOEY.

PAINTED BY CAPTAIN JAMES NICHOLLS, AUTUMN 1914.

Some in the village, only a very few now and fewer as each year goes by, remember Joey as he was. His story is written so that neither he nor those who knew him, nor the war they lived and died in, will be forgotten.

CHAPTER 1

MY EARLIEST MEMORIES ARE A CONFUSION OF HILLY fields and dark, damp stables, and rats that scampered along the beams above my head. But I remember well enough the day of the horse sale. The terror of it stayed with me all my life.

I was not yet six months old, a gangling, leggy colt who had never been farther than a few feet from his mother. We were parted that day in the terrible hubbub of the auction ring and I was never to see her again. She was a fine, working farm horse, getting on in years but with all the strength and stamina of an Irish draft horse quite evident in her fore and hindquarters. She was sold within minutes, and before I could follow her through the gates, she was whisked out of the ring. But somehow I was more difficult to dispose of. Perhaps it was the wild look in my eye as I circled the ring in a desperate search for my mother, or perhaps it was that none of the farmers and gypsies there were looking for a spindly-looking half-Thoroughbred colt. But whatever the reason, they were a long time haggling over how little I was worth before I heard the hammer go down, and I was driven out through the gates and into a pen outside.

"Not bad for three guineas, is he? Are you, my little firebrand? Not bad at all." The voice was harsh and thick with drink, and it belonged quite evidently to my owner. I shall not call him my master, for only one man was ever my master. My owner had a rope in his hand and was clambering into the pen followed by three or four of his red-faced friends. Each one carried a rope. They had taken off their hats and jackets and rolled up their sleeves, and they were all laughing as they came toward me. I had as yet been touched by no man and backed away from them until I felt the bars of the pen behind me and could go no farther. They seemed to lunge at me all at once, but they were slow and I managed to slip past them and into the middle of the pen where I turned to face them again. They had stopped laughing now. I screamed for my mother and heard her reply echoing in the far distance. It was toward that cry that I bolted, half charging, half jumping the rails so that I caught my foreleg as I tried to clamber over and was stranded there. I was grabbed roughly by the mane and tail and felt a rope tighten around my neck before I was thrown to the ground and held there with a man sitting, it seemed, on every part of me. I struggled until I was weak, kicking out violently every time I felt them relax, but they were too many and too strong for me. I felt the halter slip over my head and tighten around my neck and face. "So you're quite a fighter, are you?" said my owner, tightening the rope and smiling through gritted teeth. "I like a fighter. But I'll break you one way or the other. Quite the little fighting cock you are, but you'll be eating out of my hand quick as a twick."

I was dragged along the roads while tied on a short rope to the tailboard of a farm cart so that every twist and turn wrenched at my neck. By the time we reached the farm road and rumbled over the bridge into the stable yard that was to become my home, I was soaked with sweat, and the halter had rubbed my face raw. My one consolation as I was hauled into the stables that first evening was the knowledge that I was not alone. The old horse that had been pulling the cart all the way back from the market was led into the stable next to mine. As she went in, she stopped to look over my door and nickered gently. I was about to venture away from the back of my stable when my new owner brought his crop down on her side with such a vicious blow that I recoiled once again and huddled into the corner against the wall. "Get in there, you old rat-bag," he bellowed. "Proper nuisance you are, Zoey, and I don't want you teaching this young'un any of your old tricks." But in that short moment I had caught a glimpse of kindness and sympathy from that old mare that cooled my panic and soothed my spirit.

I was left there with no water and no food while he stumbled off across the cobbles and up into the farmhouse beyond. There was the sound of slamming doors and raised voices before I heard footsteps running back across the yard and excited voices coming closer. Two heads appeared at my door. One was that of a young boy who looked at me for a long time, considering me carefully before his face broke into a beaming smile. "Mother," he said deliberately. "That will be a wonderful and brave horse. Look how he holds his head." And then, "Look at him, Mother. He's wet through to the skin. I'll have to rub him down."

"But your father said to leave him be, Albert," said the boy's mother. "Said it'll do him good to be left alone. He told you not to touch him."

"Mother," said Albert, slipping back the bolts on the stable door. "When Father's drunk, he doesn't know what he's saying or what he's doing. He's always drunk on market days. You've told me often enough not to pay him any account when he's like that. You feed old Zoey, Mother, while I see to him. Oh, isn't he grand, Mother? He's red almost, red bay you'd call him, wouldn't you say? And that cross down his nose is perfect. Have you ever seen a horse with a white cross like that? Have you ever seen such a thing? I will ride this horse when he's ready. I will ride him everywhere, and there won't be a horse to touch him, not in the whole parish, not in the whole country."

"You're barely past thirteen, Albert," said his mother from the next stable. "He's too young and you're too young and, anyway, Father says you're not to touch him, so don't come crying to me if he catches you in there."

"But why did he buy him, Mother?" Albert asked. "It was a calf we needed, wasn't it? That's what he went into market for, wasn't it? A calf to suckle old Celandine?"

"I know, dear. Your father's not himself when he's like that," his mother said softly. "He says that Farmer Easton was bidding for the horse, and you know what he thinks of that man after that argument over the fencing. I should imagine he bought it just to deny him. Well, that's what it looks like to me."

"Well, I'm glad he did, Mother," said Albert, walking

slowly toward me, pulling off his jacket. "Drunk or not, it's the best thing he ever did."

"Don't speak like that about your father, Albert. He's been through a lot. It's not right," said his mother. But her words lacked conviction.

Albert was about the same height as me and talked so gently as he approached that I was immediately calmed and a little intrigued, and so stood where I was against the wall. I jumped at first when he touched me but could see at once that he meant me no harm. He smoothed my back first and then my neck, talking all the while about what a fine time we would have together, how I would grow up to be the smartest horse in the whole wide world, and how we would go out hunting together. After a bit, he began to rub me gently with his coat. He rubbed me until I was dry and then dabbed salt water onto my face where the skin had been rubbed raw. He brought in some sweet hay and a deep bucket of cool water. I do not believe he stopped talking the whole time. As he turned to go out of the stable, I called out to him to thank him and he seemed to understand for he smiled broadly and stroked my nose. "We'll get along, you and I," he said kindly. "I will call you Joey, only because it rhymes with Zoey, and then maybe – yes, maybe – because it suits you. I'll be out again in the morning – and don't worry, I'll look after you. I promise you that. Sweet dreams, Joey."

"You should never talk to horses, Albert," said his mother from outside. "They don't understand you. They're stupid creatures. Obstinate and stupid, that's what your father says, and he's known horses all his life."

"Father just doesn't understand them," said Albert. "I think he's frightened of them."

I went over to the door and watched Albert and his mother walking away into the darkness. I knew then that I had found a friend for life, that there was an instinctive and immediate bond of trust and affection between us. Next to me, old Zoey leaned over her door to try to touch me, but our noses could not quite meet.

CHAPTER 2

THROUGH THE LONG HARD WINTERS AND HAZY SUM-
mers that followed, Albert and I grew up together.
A yearling colt and a young boy have more in common than awkward gawkishness.

Whenever he was not at school in the village or at work
with his father on the farm, he would lead me out over the
fields and down to the flat, thistly marsh by the Torridge
River. Here on the only level ground on the farm he began
my training, just walking and trotting me up and down,
and later on lunging me, first one way and then the other.
On the way back to the farm, he would allow me to follow
him at my own speed, and I learned to come at his whistle,
not out of obedience but because I always wanted to be with
him. His whistle imitated the stuttering call of an owl — it
was a call I never refused and I would never forget.

Old Zoey, my only other companion, was often away

all day plowing, cutting, and harvesting out on the farm, so I was left on my own much of the time. Out in the fields in the summertime, this was bearable because I could always hear her working and call out to her from time to time, but shut in the loneliness of the stable in the winter, a whole day could pass without seeing or hearing a soul, unless Albert came for me.

As Albert had promised, it was he who cared for me and protected me all he could from his father, but his father did not turn out to be the monster I had expected. Most of the time he ignored me and if he did look me over, it was always from a distance. From time to time he could even be quite friendly, but I was never quite able to trust him, not after our first encounter. I would never let him come too close, and would always back off and shy away to the other end of the field and put old Zoey between us. On every Tuesday, however, Albert's father could still be relied upon to get drunk, and on his return, Albert would often find some pretext to be with me to ensure that he never came near me.

On one such autumn evening about two years after I came to the farm, Albert was up in the village church ringing the bells. As a precaution he had put me in the stable with old Zoey, as he always did on Tuesday evenings. "You'll be safer together. Father won't come in and bother you, not if you're together," he'd say, and then he'd lean over the stable door and lecture us about the intricacies of bell-ringing and how he had been given the big tenor bell because they thought he was man enough already to handle it and that in no time he'd be the biggest boy in the village. My Albert was proud of his bell-ringing prowess, and as Zoey and I stood head to tail in the darkening stable, lulled by the six bells ringing out over the dusky fields from the church, we knew he had every right to be proud. It is the noblest music, for everyone can share it – they have only to listen.

I must have been standing asleep, for I do not recall hearing him approach, but quite suddenly there was the dancing light of a lantern at the stable door and the bolts were pulled back. I thought at first it might be Albert, but the bells were still ringing, and then I heard the voice that was unmistakably that of Albert's father on a Tuesday night after market. He hung the lantern up above the door and came toward me. There was a whip in his hand, and he was staggering around the stable toward me.

"So, my proud little devil," he said, the threat in his voice quite undisguised. "I've made a bet that I can have you pulling a plow before the end of the week. Farmer Easton and the others at The George think I can't handle you. But

I'll show 'em. You've been pampered enough, and the time has come for you to earn your keep. I'm going to try some collars on you this evening, find one that fits, and then tomorrow we'll start plowing. Now we can do it the nice way or the nasty way. Give me trouble and I'll whip you till you bleed."

Old Zoey knew his mood well enough and whinnied her warning, backing off into the dark recesses of the stable, but she need not have warned me, for I sensed his intention. One look at the raised whip sent my heart thumping wildly with fear. Terrified, I knew I could not run, for there was nowhere to go, so I put my back to him, and lashed out behind me. I felt my hooves strike home. I heard a cry of pain and turned to see him crawling out of the stable door, dragging one leg stiffly behind him and muttering words of cruel vengeance.

That next morning, both Albert and his father came out together to the stables. His father was walking with a pronounced limp. They were carrying a collar each, and I could see that Albert had been crying, for his pale cheeks were stained with tears. They stood together at the stable door. I noticed with infinite pride and pleasure that my Albert was already taller than his father, whose face was drawn and lined with pain. "If your mother hadn't begged me last night, Albert, I'd have shot that horse on the spot. He could've killed me. Now I'm warning you, if that animal is not plowing straight as an arrow inside a week, he'll be sold, and that's a promise. It's up to you. You say you can deal with him, and I'll give you just one chance. He won't let me go near him. He's wild and vicious, and unless you make it your business to tame him and train him inside that week, he's going. Do you understand? That horse has to earn his keep like everyone else around here – I don't care how pretty he is – that horse has got to learn how to work. And I'll promise you another thing, Albert: if I have to lose that bet, then he has to go." He dropped the collar on the ground and turned on his heel to go.

"Father," said Albert with resolution in his voice, "I'll train Joey – I'll train him to plow all right – but you must promise never to raise a whip to him again. He can't be handled that way. I know him, Father. I know him as if he were my own brother."

"You train him, Albert, you handle him. Don't care how you do it. I don't want to know," said his father dismissively. "I'll never go near the brute again. I'd shoot him first."

But when Albert came into the stable, it was not to soothe me as he usually did nor to talk to me gently. Instead he walked up to me and looked me hard in the eye. "That was plain stupid," he said sternly. "If you want to survive, Joey, you'll have to learn. You're never to kick out at anyone ever again. He means it, Joey. He'd have shot you just like that if it hadn't been for Mother. It was Mother who saved you. He wouldn't listen to me and he never will. So never again, Joey. Never." His voice changed now, and he spoke more like himself. "We have one week, Joey, only one week to get you plowing. I know with all that Thoroughbred in you, you may think it beneath you, but that's what you're going to have to do. Old Zoey and me, we're going to train you, and it'll be very hard work – even harder for you because you're not quite the right shape for it. There's not enough of you yet. You won't much like me by the end of it, Joey. But Father means what he says. He's a man of his word. Once he's made up his mind, then that's that. He'd sell you, even shoot you rather than lose that bet, and that's for sure."

That same morning, with the mists still clinging to the fields and linked side by side to dear old Zoey in a collar that hung loose around my shoulders, I was led out onto Long Close and my training as a farm horse began. As we took the strain together for the first time, the collar rubbed at my skin and my feet sank deep into the soft ground with the effort of it. Behind, Albert was shouting almost continuously, flashing a whip at me whenever I hesitated or went off line, whenever he felt I was not giving it my best — and he knew. This was a different Albert. Gone were the gentle words and the kindnesses of the past. His voice had a harshness and a sharpness to it that wouldn't tolerate any refusal on my part. Beside me, old Zoey leaned into her collar and pulled silently, head down, digging in with her feet. For her sake and for my own sake — for Albert's, too — I leaned my weight into my collar and began to pull. I was to learn during that week the rudiments of plowing like a farm horse. Every muscle I had ached with the strain of it, but after a night's good rest stretched out in the stable I was fresh again and ready for work the next morning.

Each day as I progressed and we began to plow more as a team, Albert used the whip less and less and spoke more gently to me again, until finally at the end of the week I was sure I had all but regained his affection. Then one afternoon after we had finished the headland around Long Close, he unhitched the plow and put an arm around each of us. "It's all right now, you've done it, my beauties. You've done it," he said. "I didn't tell you, because I didn't want to put you off, but Father and Farmer Easton have been watching us from the house this afternoon." He scratched us behind the ears and smoothed our noses. "Father's won his bet and he told me at breakfast that if we finished the field today he'd forget all about the incident, and that you could stay on, Joey. So you've done it, my beauty, and I'm so proud of you I could kiss you, you old silly, but I won't do that, not with them watching. He'll let you stay now. I'm sure he will. My father is a man of his word. You can be sure of that — as long as he's sober."

It was some months later, on the way back from cutting the hay in Great Meadow along the sunken leafy road that led up into the farmyard that Albert first talked to us about the war. His whistling stopped in mid-tune. "Mother says there's likely to be a war," he said sadly. "I don't know what it's about — something about some old duke that's been shot at somewhere. Can't think why that should matter to anyone, but she says we'll be in it all the same. But it won't affect us, not down here. We'll go on just the same. At fifteen I'm too young to go, anyway — well, that's what she said. But I tell you, Joey, if there is a war I'd want to go. I think I'd make a good soldier, don't you? Look fine in a uniform, wouldn't I? And I've always wanted to march to the beat of a band. Can you imagine that, Joey? If it comes to that, you'd make a good war horse yourself, wouldn't you, if you ride as well as you pull, and I know you will. We'd make quite a pair. God help the Germans if they ever have to fight the two of us."

One hot summer evening, after a long and dusty day in the fields, I was deep into my mash and oats, with Albert still rubbing me down with straw and talking on about the abundance of good straw they'd have for the winter months, and about how good the wheat straw would be for the thatching they would be doing, when I heard his father's heavy steps coming across the yard toward us. He was calling out as he came. "Mother," he shouted. "Mother, come out, Mother." It was his sane voice, his sober voice, and was a voice that held no fear for me. "It's war, Mother. I've just heard it in the village. Postman came in this afternoon with the news. The Germans have marched into Belgium. It's certain for sure now. We declared war yesterday at eleven o'clock. We're at war with the Germans. We'll give them such a hiding they won't ever raise their fists again to anyone. Be over in a few months. It's always been the same. Just because the British lion's sleeping, they think he's dead. We'll teach them a thing or two, Mother – we'll teach them a lesson they'll never forget."

Albert had stopped brushing me and dropped the straw on the ground. We moved over toward the stable door. His mother was standing on the steps by the door of the farmhouse. She had her hand to her mouth. "Oh, dear God," she said softly. "Oh, dear God."

CHAPTER 3

G RADUALLY DURING THAT LAST SUMMER ON THE
farm, so gradually that I had hardly noticed it,
Albert had begun riding me out over the farm to
check the sheep. Old Zoey would follow along behind, and
I would stop every now and then to be sure she was still
with us. I do not even remember the first time he put a
saddle on me, but at some time he must have done so
because by the time war was declared that summer, Albert
was riding me out to the sheep each morning and almost
every evening after his work. I came to know every road
in the parish, every whispering oak tree and every bang-
ing gate. We would splash through the stream under
Innocent's Grove and thunder up Ferny Piece beyond.
With Albert riding me, there was no hanging on the reins,
no jerking on the bit in my mouth; a gentle squeeze with
the knees and a touch with his heels was enough to tell

me what he wanted of me. I think he could have ridden me even without that, so well did we come to understand each other. Whenever he was not talking to me, he would whistle or sing all the time, and that seemed somehow to reassure me.

The war hardly touched us on the farm to start with. With more straw still to turn and stack for the winter, old Zoey and I were led out every morning early into the fields to work. To our great relief, Albert had now taken over most of the horse work on the farm, leaving his father to see to the pigs and cattle, to check the sheep, and to mend fences and dig the ditches around the farm, so that we scarcely saw him for more than a few minutes each day. Yet in spite of the normality of the routine, there was a growing tension on the farm, and I began to feel an acute sense of foreboding. There would be long and heated exchanges in the yard, sometimes between Albert's father and mother, but more often, strangely enough, between Albert and his mother.

"You mustn't blame him, Albert," she said one morning, turning on him angrily outside the stable door. "He did it all for you, you know. When Lord Denton offered to sell him the farm ten years ago, he took out the mortgage so that you'd have a farm of your own when you grow up.

And it's the mortgage that worries him sick and makes him drink. So if he isn't himself from time to time you've no right to criticize him. He's not as well as he used to be, and he can't put in the work on the farm like he used to. He's more than fifty, you know – children don't think of their fathers as being old or young. And it's the war, too. The war worries him, Albert. He's worried prices will be falling, and I think in his heart of hearts he feels he should be soldiering in France – but he's too old for that. You've got to try to understand him, Albert. He deserves that much."

"You don't drink, Mother," Albert replied vehemently. "And you've got worries just like he has and, anyway, if you did drink, you wouldn't yell at me like he does. I do all the work I can, and more, and still he never stops complaining that this isn't done and that isn't done. He complains every time I take Joey out in the evening. He doesn't even want me to go off bell-ringing once a week. It's not reasonable, Mother."

"I know that, Albert," his mother said more gently now, taking his hand in both of hers. "But you must try to see the good in him. He's a good man – he really is. You remember him that way, too, don't you?"

"Yes, Mother. I remember him like that," Albert acknowledged, "but if only he wouldn't keep complaining about

Joey like he does. After all, Joey works for his living now and he has to have time off to enjoy himself, just like I do."

"Of course, dear," she said, taking his elbow and walking him up toward the farmhouse, "but you know how he feels about Joey, don't you? He bought him out of spite and has regretted it ever since. As he says, we really only need one horse for the farmwork, and that horse of yours eats money. That's what worries him. Farmers and horses, it's always the same. My father was like that, too. But he'll come around if you're kind to him – I know he will."

But Albert and his father scarcely spoke to each other anymore those days, and Albert's mother was used more and more by both as a go-between, as a negotiator. It was on a Wednesday morning with the war but a few weeks old, that Albert's mother was again arbitrating between them in the yard outside. As usual, Albert's father had come home drunk from the market the night before. He said he had forgotten to take back the saddleback boar they had borrowed to mate with the sows and gilts. He had told Albert to do it, but Albert had objected strongly and an argument was brewing. Albert's father said that he "had business to attend to" and Albert maintained he had the stables to clean out.

"Won't take you but half an hour, dear, to drive the boar

back down the valley to Fursden," Albert's mother said swiftly, trying to soften the inevitable.

"All right, then," Albert conceded, as he always did when his mother intervened, for he hated to upset her. "I'll do it for you, Mother. But only on condition I can take Joey out this evening. I want to hunt him this winter and I have to get him fit." Albert's father stayed silent and thin-lipped, and I noticed then that he was looking straight at me. Albert turned, patted me gently on the nose, picked up a stick from the pile of tinder by the woodshed, and made his way down toward the piggery. A few minutes later, I saw him driving the great black-and-white boar out down the farm track toward the road. I called out after him but he did not turn around.

Now if Albert's father came into the stable at all, it was always to lead out old Zoey. He left me alone these days. He would throw a saddle onto Zoey in the yard and ride out onto the hills above the farmhouse to check the sheep. So it was nothing special when he came into the stable that morning and led Zoey out. But when he came back into the stable afterward and began to sweet-talk me and held out a bucket of sweet-smelling oats, I was immediately suspicious. But the oats and my own inquisitiveness overcame my better judgment, and he was able to slip a halter over my head before I could pull away. His voice, however, was unusually gentle and kind as he tightened the halter and reached out slowly to stroke my neck. "You'll be all right, old son," he said softly. "You'll be all right. They'll look after you – they promised they would. And I need the money, Joey; I need the money bad."

CHAPTER 4

YING A LONG ROPE TO THE HALTER, HE WALKED ME OUT of the stable. I went with him because Zoey was out there looking back over her shoulder at me and I was always happy to go anywhere and with anyone as long as she was with me. All the while I noticed that Albert's father was speaking in a hushed voice and looking around him like a thief.

He must have known that I would follow old Zoey because he roped me up to her saddle and led us both quietly out of the yard down the path and over the bridge. Once in the road, he mounted Zoey swiftly and we trotted up the hill and into the village. He never spoke a word to either of us. I knew the road well enough, of course, for I had been there often enough with Albert, and indeed I loved going there because there were always other horses to meet and people to see. It was in the village only a short time before that I had met my first motorcar outside the post office and had stiffened with fear as it rattled past, but I had stood steady, and I remember that Albert had made a big fuss over me after that. But now, as we neared the village, I could see that several motorcars were parked around the green, and there was a greater gathering of men and horses than I had ever seen. Excited as I was, I remember that a sense of deep apprehension came over me as we trotted up into the village.

There were men in khaki uniforms everywhere, and then, as Albert's father dismounted and led us up past the church toward the green, a military band struck up a rousing, pounding march. The pulse of the great bass-drum beat out through the village, and there were children everywhere, some marching up and down with broomsticks over their shoulders and some leaning out of windows waving flags.

As we approached the flagpole in the center of the green where the Union Jack hung limp in the sun against the white pole, an officer pushed through the crowd toward us. He was tall and elegant in his jodhpurs and military belt, with a silver sword at his side. He shook Albert's father by the hand. 'I told you I'd come, Captain Nicholls, sir," said Albert's father. "It's because I need the money, you understand. Wouldn't part with a horse like this 'less I had to."

"Well, Farmer," said the officer, nodding his appreciation as he looked me over. "I'd thought you'd be exaggerating when we talked in The George last evening. 'Finest horse in the parish,' you said, but then everyone says that. But this one is different – I can see that." And he smoothed my neck gently and scratched me behind my ears. Both his hand and his voice were kind, and I did not shrink away from him. "You're right, Farmer. He'd make a fine mount for my regiment and we'd be proud to have him – I wouldn't mind using him myself. No, I wouldn't mind at all. If he turns out to be all he looks, then he'd suit me well enough. Fine-looking animal, no question about it."

"Forty pounds you'll pay me, Captain Nicholls, like you promised yesterday?" Albert's father said in a voice that was unnaturally low, almost as if he did not want to be heard by anyone else. "I can't let him go for a penny less. A man's got to live."

"That's what I promised you last evening, Farmer," Captain Nicholls said, opening my mouth and examining my teeth. "He's a fine young horse – strong neck, sloping shoulder, straight fetlocks. Done much work has he? Have you taken him hunting?"

"My son rides him every day," said Albert's father. He tells me that he goes like a racer and jumps like a hunter."

"Well," said the officer, "as long as our vet passes him as fit and sound in wind and limb, you'll have your forty pounds, as we agreed."

"I can't be long, sir," Albert's father said, glancing back over his shoulder. "I have to get back. I have my work to see to."

"Well, we're busy recruiting in the village as well as buying," said the officer. "But we'll be as quick as we can for you. True, there's a lot more good men volunteers than there are good horses in these parts, and the vet doesn't have to examine the men, does he? You wait here, I'll only be a few minutes."

Captain Nicholls led me away through the archway opposite the pub and into a large yard where there were men in white coats and a uniformed clerk sitting down at a table taking notes. I thought I heard old Zoey calling after me, so I shouted back to reassure her for I felt no fear at this moment. I was too interested in what was going on around me. The officer talked to me gently as we walked away, so I went along almost eagerly. The vet, a small, bustling man with a bushy black moustache, prodded me all over, lifted each of my feet to examine them – which I objected to – and then peered into my eyes and my mouth, sniffing at my breath. Then I was trotted around and around the yard before he pronounced me a perfect specimen. "Sound as a bell. Fit for anything, cavalry or artillery," were the words he used. "No splints, not lame, good feet and teeth. Buy him, Captain," he said. "He's a good one."

I was led back to Albert's father who took the offered money from Captain Nicholls, stuffing it quickly into his trouser pocket. "You'll look after him, sir?" he said. "You'll see he comes to no harm? My son's very fond of him, you see." He reached out and brushed my nose with his hand. There were tears filling his eyes. At that moment he became almost a likable man to me. "You'll be all right, old son," he whispered to me. "You won't understand and neither will Albert, but unless I sell you, I can't keep up with the mortgage and we'll lose the farm. I've treated you bad – I've treated everyone bad. I know it and I'm sorry for it." And he walked away from me, leading Zoey behind him. His head was lowered, and he looked suddenly like a shrunken man.

It was then that I fully realized I was being abandoned, and I began to neigh, a high-pitched cry of pain and anxiety that shrieked out through the village. Even old Zoey, obedient and placid as she always was, stopped and would not be moved on no matter how hard Albert's father pulled her. She turned, tossed up her head, and shouted her fare-well. But her cries became weaker and she was finally dragged away and out of my sight. Kind hands tried to contain me and to console me, but I was inconsolable.

I had just about given up all hope, when I saw my Albert running toward me through the crowd, his face red with exertion. The band had stopped playing, and the entire village looked on as he came up to me and put his arms around my neck.

"He's sold him, hasn't he?" he said quietly, looking up at Captain Nicholls who was holding me. "Joey is my horse. He's my horse and he always will be, no matter who buys him. I can't stop my father from selling him, but if Joey goes with you, I go. I want to join up and stay with him."

"You've got the right spirit for a soldier, young man," said the officer, taking off his peaked cap and wiping his brow with the back of his hand. He had black curly hair and a kind, open look on his face. "You've got the spirit, but you haven't got the years. You're too young and you know it. Seventeen's the youngest age we take. Come back in a year or so and then we'll see."

"I look seventeen," Albert said, almost pleading. "I'm bigger than most seventeen-year-olds." But even as he spoke, he could see he was getting nowhere. "You won't

take me then, sir? Not even as a stable boy? I'll do anything – anything."

"What's your name, young man?" Captain Nicholls asked.

"Narracott, sir, Albert Narracott."

"Well, Mr. Narracott. I'm sorry I can't help you." The officer shook his head and replaced his cap. "I'm sorry, young
man, regulations. But don't you worry about your Joey. I
shall take good care of him until you're ready to join us.
You've done a fine job with him. You should be proud of
him – he's a fine, fine horse, but your father needed the
money for the farm, and a farm won't run without money.
You must know that. I like your spirit, so when you're old
enough, you must come and join the cavalry. We need
men like you, and it will be a long war I fear, longer than
people think. Mention my name. I'm Captain Nicholls,
and I'd be proud to have you with us."

"There's no way, then?" Albert asked. "There's nothing I
can do?"

"Nothing," said Captain Nicholls. "Your horse belongs to
the army now, and you're too young to join up. Don't you
worry – we'll look after him. I'll take personal care of him,
and that's a promise."

Albert rubbed my nose for me as he often did and
stroked my ears. He was trying to smile but could not. "I'll

find you again, you old silly," he said quietly. "Wherever you are, I'll find you, Joey. Take good care of him, please, sir, till I find him again. There's not another horse like him, not in the whole world — you'll find that out. Say you promise?"

"I promise," said Captain Nicholls. "I'll do everything I can." And Albert turned and went away through the crowd until I could see him no more.

CHAPTER 5

I N THE FEW SHORT WEEKS BEFORE I WENT OFF TO WAR, I WAS
to be changed from a working farm horse into a cavalry mount. It was no easy transformation, for I resented
deeply the tight discipline of the riding school and the
hard hot hours out on maneuvers out in the fields. Back at
home with Albert, I had reveled in the long rides along the
roads and over the fields, and the heat and the flies had
not seemed to matter; I had loved the aching days of plowing alongside Zoey, but that was because there had been a
bond between us of trust and devotion. Now there were
endless tedious hours circling the school. Gone was the
gentle snaffle bit that I was so used to, and in its place was
an uncomfortable, cumbersome barbed bit that pinched the
corners of my mouth and infuriated me beyond belief.

But it was my rider that I disliked more than anything
in my new life. Corporal Samuel Perkins was a hard, gritty

little man, an ex-jockey whose only pleasure in life seemed to be the power he could exert over a horse. He was universally feared by all troopers and horses alike. Even the officers, I felt, went in trepidation of him, for it seemed he knew all there was to know about horses and had the experience of a lifetime behind him. And he rode hard and heavy-handedly. With him, the whip and the spurs were not just for show.

He would never beat me or lose his temper with me; indeed, sometimes when he was grooming me I think he quite liked me, and I certainly felt for him a degree of respect, but this was based on fear and not love. In my anger and unhappiness, I tried several times to throw him off but never succeeded. His knees had a grip of iron, and he seemed instinctively to know what I was about to do.

My only consolation in those early days of training were the visits of Captain Nicholls every evening to the stables. He alone seemed to have the time to come and talk to me as Albert had done before. Sitting on an upside-down bucket in the corner of my stable, a sketchbook on his knees, he would draw me as he talked. "I've done a few sketches of you now," he said one evening, "and when I've finished this one, I'll be ready to paint a picture of you. It won't be Stubbs — it'll be better than Stubbs because Stubbs never had a horse as beautiful as you to paint. I can't take it with me to France – there would no point, right? So I'm going to send it off to your friend Albert, just so that he'll know that I meant what I said when I promised I would look after you." He kept looking up and down at me as he worked, and I longed to tell him how much I wished he would take over my training himself and how hard the Corporal was and how my sides hurt and my feet hurt. "To be honest with you, Joey, I hope this war will be over before he's old enough to join us because – you mark my words – it's going to be nasty, very nasty indeed. Back in the mess hall, they're all talking about how they'll get the Germans, how the cavalry will smash through them and throw them clear back to Berlin before Christmas. It's just Jamie and me – we're the only ones that don't agree, Joey. We have our doubts, I can tell you that. We have our doubts. None of them in there seem to have heard of machine guns and artillery. I tell you, Joey, one machine gun operated right could wipe out an entire squadron of the best cavalry in the world – German or British. I mean, look what happened to the Light Brigade at Balaclava when they took on the Russian guns – none of them seem to remember that. And the French learned the lesson in the Franco-Prussian War. But you can't say anything to them, Joey. If you do, they call you a defeatist, or some such rubbish. I honestly think that some of them in there only want to win this war if the cavalry can win it."

He stood up, tucked the sketchbook under his arm, and came over toward me and scratched me behind the ears. "You like that, boy, don't you? Under all that fire and brimstone, you're an old softy at heart. Come to think of it, we have a lot in common, you and I. First, we don't much like it here and would rather be somewhere else. Second, neither of us ever been to war — never even heard a shot fired in anger, have we? I just hope I'm up to it when the time comes — that's what worries me more than anything, Joey. Because I tell you, and I haven't even told Jamie this — I'm frightened as hell, so you'd better have enough courage for the two of us."

A door banged open across the yard and I heard the familiar sound of boots, crisp on the cobbles. It was Corporal Samuel Perkins passing along the lines of stables on his evening rounds, stopping at each one to check until, at last, he came to mine. "Good evening, sir," he said, saluting smartly. "Sketching again?"

"Doing my best, Corporal," said Captain Nicholls. "Doing my best to do him justice. Is he not the finest mount in the entire squadron? I've never seen a horse so well put together as he is, have you?"

"Oh, he's special enough to look at, sir," said the Corporal of Horse. Even his voice put my ears back; there was a thin, acid tone to it that I dreaded. "I grant you that, but looks aren't everything, are they, sir? There's always more to a horse than meets the eye, isn't that right, sir? How shall I put it, sir?"

"However you like, Corporal," said Captain Nicholls somewhat frostily, "but be careful what you say, for that's my horse you're speaking about, so take care."

"Let's say, I feel he has a mind of his own. Yes, let's put it that way. He's good enough out on maneuvers — a real stayer, one of the very best — but inside the school, sir, he's a devil, and a strong devil, too. Never been properly schooled, sir, you can tell that. He's a farm horse, he is, and farm-trained. If he's to be a cavalry horse, sir, he'll have to learn to accept the disciplines. He has to learn to obey instantly and instinctively. You don't want a prima donna under you when the bullets start flying."

"Fortunately, Corporal," said Captain Nicholls, "fortunately this war will be fought out of doors and not indoors. I asked you to train Joey because I think you are the best man for the job – there's no one better in the squadron. But perhaps you should ease up on him just a bit. You've got to remember where he came from. He's a willing soul – he just needs a bit of gentle persuasion, that's all. But keep it gentle, Corporal, keep it gentle. I don't want him soured. This horse is going to carry me through the war and, with any luck, out the other side of it. He's special to me, Corporal – you know that. So make sure you look after him as if he were your own, won't you? We leave for France in under a week now. If I had the time, I'd be schooling him myself, but I'm far too busy trying to turn troopers into mounted infantry. A horse may carry you through, Corporal, but he can't do your fighting for you. And some of them still think they'll only need their sabers when they get out there. Some of them really believe that flashing their sabers around will frighten the Germans all the way home. I tell you, they have got to learn to shoot straight – we'll all have to learn to shoot straight if we want to win this war."

"Yes, sir," said the corporal with a new respect in his voice. He was more meek and mild now than I had ever seen him.

"And, Corporal," said Captain Nicholls walking toward the stable door, "I'd be obliged if you'd give Joey a little extra food sometime. He's lost a bit of condition, gone back a bit I'd say. I shall be taking him out myself on final maneuvers in two or three days, and I want him fit and shining. He has to look the best in the squadron."

It was only in that last week of my military education that I began at last to settle into the work. Corporal Samuel Perkins seemed less harsh toward me after that evening. He used the spurs less and gave me more rein. We did less work now in the school and more formation work on the open fields outside the camp. I took the Weymouth bit more readily now and began to play with it between my teeth as I had always done with the snaffle. I began to appreciate the good food and the grooming and the buffing up, all the unending attention and care that was devoted to me. As the days passed I began to think less and less of the farm and old Zoey and of my early life. But Albert, his face and his voice, stayed clear in my mind despite the unerring routine of the work that was turning me imperceptibly into an army horse.

By the time Captain Nicholls came to take me out on those last maneuvers before we went to war, I was already quite resigned to, even contented in, my new life. Dressed now in field-service marching order, Captain Nicholls weighed heavy on my back as the entire regiment moved out onto Salisbury Plain. I remember mostly the heat and the flies that day because there were hours of standing about in the sun waiting for things to happen. Then, with the evening sun spreading and dying along the flat horizon, the entire regiment lined up in echelon for the charge, the climax of our last maneuvers.

The order was given to draw swords and we walked forward. As we waited for the bugle calls, the air was electric with anticipation. It passed between every horse and his rider, between horse and horse, between trooper and trooper. I felt inside me a surge of such excitement that I found it difficult to contain myself. Captain Nicholls was leading his troops and alongside him rode his friend Captain Jamie Stewart on a horse I had never seen before. He was a tall, shining black stallion. As we walked forward I glanced up at him and caught his eye. He seemed to acknowledge it briefly. The walk moved into a trot and then into a canter. I heard the bugles blow and caught sight of his saber pointing over my right ear. Captain Nicholls leaned forward in the saddle and urged me into a gallop. The thunder and the dust and the roar of men's voice in my ears took a hold of me and held me at a pitch of exhilaration I had never before experienced. I flew over the ground way ahead of the rest of them except for one. The only horse to stay with me was the shining black stallion. Although nothing was said between Captain Nicholls and Captain Stewart, I felt it was suddenly important that I should not allow this horse to get ahead of me. One look told me that he felt the same, for there was a grim determination in his eyes and his brow was furrowed with concentration. When we overran the "enemy" position, it was all our riders could do to bring us to a halt, and finally we stood nose to nose, blowing and panting with both captains breathless with exertion.

"You see, Jamie, I told you so," said Captain Nicholls, and there was such pride in his voice as he spoke. "This is the horse I was telling you about – found deep in Devon – and if we had gone on much longer, your Topthorn would have been struggling to stay with him. You can't deny it."

Topthorn and I looked warily at each other at first. He was half a hand or more taller than me, a huge sleek horse that held his head with majestic dignity. He was the first horse I had ever come across that I felt could challenge me for strength, but there was also a kindness in his eye that held no threat for me.

"My Topthorn is the finest mount in this regiment or any other," said Captain Jamie Stewart. "Joey might be faster and, all right, I'll grant you he looks as good as any horse I've ever seen, but there's no one to match my Topthorn for stamina – why, he could have gone on forever and ever. He's an eight-horsepower horse, and that's a fact."

On the way back to the barracks that evening, the two officers debated the virtues of their respective horses, while Topthorn and I plodded along shoulder to shoulder, heads hanging, our strength sapped by the sun and the long gallop. We were stabled side by side that night, and again on the boat the next day we found ourselves together in the bowels of the converted ocean liner that was to carry us off to France and away to the war.

CHAPTER 6

ALL ABOUT US ON THE SHIP, THERE WAS AN AIR OF great exuberance and expectancy. The soldiers were buoyant with optimism, as if they were embarking on some great military picnic; it seemed none of them had a care in the world. As they tended us in our stalls, the troopers joked and laughed together as I had never heard them before. And we were to need their confidence around us, for it was a stormy crossing and many of us became overwrought and apprehensive as the ship tossed wildly in the sea. Some of us kicked out at our stalls in a desperate effort to break free and to find ground that did not pitch and plunge under our feet, but the troopers were always there to hold us steady and to comfort us.

My comfort, however, came not from Corporal Samuel Perkins, who came to hold my head through the worst of it; for even when he patted me, he did it in such a peremptory fashion that I did not feel he meant it. My comfort came from Topthorn, who remained calm throughout. He would lean his great head over the stall and let me rest on his neck while I tried to obliterate from my mind the sinking surge of the ship and the noise of uncontrolled terror from the horses all around me.

But the moment we docked, the mood changed. The horses recovered their composure with solid, still land under their hooves once more, but the troopers fell silent and somber as we walked past unending lines of wounded waiting to board the ship back to England. As we disembarked and were led away along the quayside, Captain Nicholls walked by my head turning his eyes out to sea so that no one should notice the tears in them. The wounded were everywhere – on stretchers, on crutches, in open ambulances, and etched on every man was the look of wretched misery and pain. They tried to put a brave face on it, but even the jokes and quips they shouted out as we passed were heavy with gloom and sarcasm. No sergeant major, no enemy barrage could have silenced a body of soldiers as effectively as that terrible sight, for here for the first time the men saw for themselves the kind of war they were going into, and there was not a single man in the squadron who seemed prepared for it.

Once out into the flat, open country, the squadron threw off its unfamiliar shroud of despondency and regained its jocular spirits. The men sang again in their saddles and laughed among themselves. It was to be a long, long march through the dust, all that day and the next. We would stop once every hour for a few minutes and would ride on until dusk before making camp near a village and always by a stream or a river. They cared for us well on that march, often dismounting and walking beside us to give us the rest we needed. But sweetest of all were the full buckets of cooling, quenching water they would bring us whenever we stopped beside a stream. Topthorn, I noticed, always shook his head in the water before he started to drink so that alongside him I was showered all over my face and neck with cooling water.

The mounts were tethered in horse lines out in the open as we had been on maneuvers back in England. So we were already hardened to living outdoors. But it was colder now as the damp mists of autumn fell each evening and chilled us where we stood. We had plenty of fodder morning and evening, a generous ration of corn from our nose bags, and we grazed whenever we could. Like the men, we had to learn to live off the land as much as possible.

Every hour of the march brought us nearer the distant

thunder of the guns, and at night now the horizon would be bright with orange flashes from one end to the other. I had heard the crack of rifle fire before back at the barracks, and this had not upset me one bit, but the growling crescendo of the big guns sent tremors of fear along my back and broke my sleep into a succession of jagged nightmares. But whenever I woke, dragged back to consciousness by the guns, I found Topthorn was always by me and would breathe his courage into me to support me. It was a slow baptism of fire for me, but without Topthorn I think I should never have become accustomed to the guns, for the fury and the violence of the thunder as we came ever nearer to the front line seemed to sap my strength as well as my spirits.

On the march, Topthorn and I walked always together, side by side, for Captain Nicholls and Captain Stewart were rarely apart. They seemed somehow separate in spirit from their heartier fellow officers. The more I got to know Captain Nicholls, the more I liked him. He rode me as Albert had, with a gentle hand and a firm grip of the knees, so that despite his size – and he was a big man – he was always light on me. And there was always some warm word of encouragement or gratitude after a long ride. This was a welcome contrast to Corporal Samuel Perkins, who had ridden me so hard while in training. I caught sight of him from time to time and pitied the horse he rode.

Captain Nicholls did not sing or whistle as Albert had, but he talked to me from time to time when we were alone together. It appeared no one really knew where the enemy was. That he was advancing and that we were retreating was not in doubt. We were supposed to try to ensure that the enemy did not outflank us – we did not want the enemy to get between us and the sea and turn the flank of the whole British expeditionary force. But the squadron first had to find the enemy and they were never anywhere to be seen. We scoured the countryside for days before finally blundering into them – and that was a day I shall never forget: the day of our first battle.

Rumor rippled back along the column that the enemy had been sighted, a battalion of infantry on the march. They were out in the open a mile or so away, hidden from us by a long thick grove of oaks that ran alongside the road. The orders rang out: "Forward! Form squadron column! Draw swords!" As one, the men reached down and grasped their swords from their sheaths, and the air flickered with bright steel before the blades settled on the troopers' shoulders. "Squadron, right shoulder!" came the command, and we walked in line abreast into the woods.

I felt Captain Nicholls's knees close right around me and he loosened the reins. His body was taut and for the first time he felt heavy on my back. "Easy, Joey," he said softly. "Easy now. Don't get excited. We'll come out of this all right, don't you worry."

I turned to look at Topthorn, who was already up on his toes ready for the trot that we knew was to come. I moved instinctively closer to him, and then, as the bugle sounded, we charged out of the shade of the woods and into the sunlight of battle.

The gentle squeak of leather, the jingling harness, and the noise of hastily barked orders were drowned now by the pounding of hooves and the shout of the troopers as we galloped down on the enemy in the valley below us. Out of the corner of my eye, I was aware of the glint of Captain Nicholls's heavy sword. I felt his spurs in my side, and I heard his battle cry. I saw the gray soldiers ahead of us raise their rifles and heard the death rattle of a machine gun, and then quite suddenly I found that I had no rider, that I had no weight on my back anymore, and that I was alone out in front of the squadron. Topthorn was no longer beside me, but with horses behind me I knew there was only one way to gallop, and that was forward. Blind terror drove me on, with my flying stirrups whipping me into a frenzy. With no rider to carry, I reached the kneeling rifle-men first, and they scattered as I came upon them.

I ran on until I found myself alone and away from the noise of the battle, and I would never have stopped at all had I not found Topthorn once more beside me with Captain Stewart leaning over to gather up my reins before leading me back to the battlefield.

We had won, I heard it said, but horses lay dead and dying everywhere. More than a quarter of the squadron had been lost in that one action. It had all been so quick and so deadly. A cluster of gray-uniformed prisoners had been taken and they huddled together now under the trees while the squadron regrouped and exchanged extravagant reminiscences of a victory that had happened almost by accident rather than by design.

I never saw Captain Nicholls again, and that was a great and terrible sadness for me, for he had been a kind and gentle man and had cared for me well, as he had promised. As I was to learn, there were few enough such good men in the world. "He'd have been proud of you, Joey," said Captain Stewart as he led me back to the horse lines with Topthorn. "He'd have been proud of you, the way you kept going out there. He died leading that charge and you fin-ished it for him. He'd have been proud of you."

Topthorn stood over me that night as we camped on the edge of the woods. We looked out together over the moon-lit valley, and I longed for home. Only the occasional coughing and stamping of the sentries broke the still of the night. The guns were silent at last. Topthorn sank down beside me and we slept.

CHAPTER 7

I T WAS JUST AFTER REVEILLE THE NEXT MORNING, AND WE were rummaging around in our nose bags for the last of our oats, when I saw Captain Jamie Stewart striding along the horse lines toward us. Behind him, swamped in a vast greatcoat and a peaked cap, trailed a young trooper I had never seen before. He was pink-faced and young under his hat and reminded me at once of Albert. I sensed that he was nervous of me, for his approach was hesitant and reluctant.

Captain Stewart felt Topthorn's ears and stroked his soft muzzle as he always did the first thing in the morning, and then reaching across he patted me gently on the neck. "Well, Trooper Warren, here he is," said Captain Stewart. "Come closer, Trooper, he won't bite. This is Joey. This horse belonged to the best friend I ever had, so you look after him, d'you hear?" His tone was firm but not unsympathetic.

"And, Trooper, I will be able to keep my eye on you all the time because these two horses are inseparable. They are the two best horses in the squadron, and they know it." He stepped closer to me and lifted my forelock clear of my face. "Joey," he whispered. "You take care of him. He's only a young boy and he's had a rough ride in this war so far."

So when the squadron moved out of the wood that morning I found I could no longer walk alongside Topthorn as I had before with Captain Nicholls, but was now just one of the troop following behind the officers in a long column of troopers. But whenever we stopped to feed or drink, Trooper Warren was careful to walk me over to where Topthorn stood so that we could be together.

Trooper Warren was not a good horseman – I could tell that the minute he mounted me. He was always tense and rode me heavy in the saddle like a sack of potatoes. He had neither the experience and confidence of Corporal Samuel Perkins nor the finesse and sensitivity of Captain Nicholls. He rocked unevenly in the saddle and rode me always on too tight a rein so that I was forced to toss my head continuously to loosen it. But once out of the saddle, he was the gentlest of men. He was meticulous and kind in his grooming and attended at once to my frequent and painful saddle sores, chafings, and leg swellings to which I was particularly prone. He cared for me as no one had since I left home. Over the next few months it was his loving attention that was to keep me alive.

There were a few minor skirmishes during that first autumn of the war, but as Captain Nicholls had predicted, we were used less and less as cavalry and more as transport for mounted infantry. Whenever we came across the enemy, the squadron would dismount, drawing their rifles from their buckets, and the horses would be left behind out of sight under the care of a few troopers, so that we never saw any action ourselves but heard the distant crackle of rifle fire and the rattle of machine guns. When the troop returned and the squadron moved off again, there were always one or two horses without riders.

We would be on the march for hours and days on end, it seemed. Then, suddenly a motorcycle would roar past us through the dust and there would be the barked commands and the shrill call of the bugles and the squadron would swing off the road and into action once more.

It was during these long, stifling marches and during the cold nights that followed that Trooper Warren began to talk to me. He told me how in the same action in which Captain Nicholls had been killed, his horse had been shot down from beneath him, and how only a few weeks before he had been an apprentice blacksmith with his father. Then the war had broken out. He did not want to join up, he said, but the squire of the village had spoken to his father, and his father, who rented his house and his blacksmith shop from the squire, had no option but to send him off to war, and since he had grown up around horses he volunteered to join the cavalry. "I tell you, Joey," he said one evening as he was picking out my hooves, "I tell you I never thought I would get on a horse again after that first battle. Strange thing is, Joey, that it wasn't the shooting — somehow I didn't mind that. It was just the idea of riding a horse again that terrified the life out of me. Wouldn't think that possible, would you? Not with me being a blacksmith and all. Still, I'm over it now, and you've done that for me, Joey. Given me back my confidence. Feel I can do anything now. Feel like one of those knights in armor when I'm up on you."

Then, with the onset of winter, the rain came down in sheets. It was refreshing at first and a welcome break from the dust and the flies, but soon the fields and paths turned to mud beneath us. The squadron could no longer camp in the dry because there was no shelter, and so both man and horse were constantly soaked to the skin. There was little or no protection from the driving rain, and at night we stood now up to our fetlocks in cold, oozing mud. But Trooper Warren looked after me with great devotion, finding shelter for me wherever and whenever he could, rubbing some warmth into me with wisps of dry straw whenever he could find it and ensuring that I always got a good ration of oats in my nose bag to keep me going. As the weeks passed, his pride in my strength and stamina became obvious to everyone, as did my affection for him. *If only,* I thought, *if only he could just groom me and care for me and someone else could ride me.*

My Trooper Warren would talk a great deal about how the war was going. We were, he said, to be withdrawn to reserve camps behind our own lines. The armies, it appeared, had pounded each other to a standstill in the mud and had dug in. The dugouts had soon become trenches, and the trenches had joined one another, zigzagging across the country from the sea to Switzerland. In the spring, he said, we would be needed again to break the deadlock. The cavalry could go where the infantry could not and were fast enough to overrun the trenches. We'd show the infantry how to do it, he said. But there was the winter to survive before the ground became hard enough again for the cavalry to be used effectively.

Topthorn and I spent the winter sheltering each other as best we could from the snow and the sleet, while only a few miles away we could hear the guns pounding each other day and night incessantly. We saw the cheery soldiers smiling under their metal hats as they marched off to the front line, whistling and singing and joking as they went, and we watched the remnants struggling back haggard and silent under their dripping capes in the rain.

Every once in a while Trooper Warren would receive a letter from home and he would read it out to me in a guarded whisper in case anyone else should overhear. The letters were all from his mother, and they all said much the same thing.

"My dear Charlie," he would read. *"Your Father hopes you are well, and so do I. We missed having you with us at Christmas — the table in the kitchen seemed empty without you. But your little brother helps when he can with the work and Father says he's coming on well, even though he's still a bit little and not strong enough yet to hold the farm horses. Minnie Whittle, that old widow from Hanniford Farm, died in her sleep last week. She was eighty, so she can't grumble at that, though I expect she would if she could. She was always the world's worst grumbler, do you remember? Well, son, that's about all our news. Your Sally from the village sends her best and says to tell*

you that she'll be writing soon. Keep safe, dearest boy, and come home soon.

Your loving Mother

But Sally won't write, Joey, because she can't – well not very well, anyway. But just as soon as this war's over and finished with, I'll get back home and marry her. I've grown up with her, Joey, known her all my life. S'pose I know her almost as well as I know myself, and I like her a lot better."

Trooper Warren broke the terrible monotony of that winter. He lifted my spirits and I could see that Topthorn too welcomed every visit he made to the horse lines. He never knew how much good he did us. During that awful winter, so many of the horses went off to the veterinary hospital and never came back. Like all army horses, our coats were clipped like hunters so that all our lower quarters were exposed to the mud and rain. The weaker ones among us suffered first, for they had little resilience and went downhill fast. But Topthorn and I came through to the spring, Topthorn surviving a severe cough that shook his whole massive frame as if it were trying to tear the life out of him from the inside. It was Captain Stewart who saved him, feeding him a hot mash and covering him as best he could in the bleakest weather.

And then, one ice-cold night in early spring, with frost lying on our backs, the troopers came to the horse lines unexpectedly early. It was before dawn. There had been a night of incessant heavy barrage and there was a new bustle and excitement in the camp. This was not one of the routine exercises we had come to expect. The troopers came along the horse lines in full-service gear, each equipped with two bandoliers, respiratory shoulder bag, rifle, and sword. We were saddled up and moved silently out of the camp and onto the road. The troopers talked of the battle ahead and all the frustrations and irritations of imposed idleness vanished as they sang in the saddle. And my Trooper Warren was singing along with them as lustily as any of them. In the cold gray of the night, the squadron joined the regiment in the remnants of a little ruined village peopled only by cats, and waited there for an hour until the pale light of dawn crept over the horizon. Still the guns bellowed out their fury and the ground shook beneath us. We passed the field hospitals and the light guns before trotting over the support trenches to catch our first sight of the battlefield. Desolation and destruction were everywhere. Not a building was left intact. Not a blade of grass grew in the torn and ravaged soil. The singing around me stopped and we moved on in ominous silence and out over the trenches that were crammed with men, their bayonets fixed to their rifles. They gave us a sporadic cheer as we clattered over the boards and out into the wilderness of no-man's-land, into a wilderness of wire and shell holes and the terrible litter of war. Suddenly the guns stopped firing overhead. We were through the wire. The squadron fanned out in a wide, uneven echelon, and the bugle sounded. I felt the spurs biting into my sides and moved up alongside Topthorn as we broke into a trot. "Do me proud, Joey," said Trooper Warren, drawing his sword. "Do me proud."

CHAPTER 8

FOR JUST A FEW SHORT MOMENTS, WE MOVED FORWARD at the trot as we had done in training. In the eerie silence of no-man's-land, all that could be heard was the jingle of the harness and the snorting of the horses. We picked our way around the craters, keeping our line as best we could. Up ahead of us at the top of a gentle sloping hill were the battered remnants of a woods, and just below a hideous, rusting roll of barbed wire that stretched out along the horizon as far as the eye could see.

"Wire," I heard Trooper Warren whisper through his teeth. "Oh, God, Joey, they said the wire would be gone. They said the guns would deal with the wire. Oh, my God!"

We were cantering now, and still there was no sound nor sight of any enemy. The troopers were shouting at an invisible foe, leaning over their horses' necks, their sabers stretched out in front of them. I galvanized myself into a gallop to keep up with Topthorn, and as I did, so the first terrible shells fell among us and the machine guns opened up. The bedlam of battle had begun. All around me, men cried and fell to the ground, and horses reared and screamed in an agony of fear and pain. The ground erupted on either side of me, throwing horses and riders clear into the air. The shells whined and roared overhead, and every explosion seemed like an earthquake to us. But the squadron galloped on inexorably through it all toward the wire at the top of the hill, and I went with them.

On my back, Trooper Warren held me in an iron grip with his knees. I stumbled once and felt him lose a stirrup, and slowed so that he could find it again. Topthorn was still ahead of me, his head up, his tail whisking from side to side. I found more strength in my legs and charged after him. Trooper Warren prayed aloud as he rode, but his prayers soon turned to curses as he saw the carnage around him. Only a few horses reached the wire, and Topthorn and I were among them. There were indeed a few holes blasted through the wire by our bombardment so that some of us could find a way through, and we came at last upon the first line of enemy trenches, but they were empty. The firing came now from higher up in among the trees, and so the squadron, or what was left of it, regrouped and galloped up into the woods, only to be met by a line of hidden wire in among the trees. Some of the horses ran into the wire before they could be stopped, and stuck there, their riders trying feverishly to extract them. I saw one trooper dismount deliberately once he saw his horse was caught. He pulled out his rifle and shot his mount before falling dead himself on the wire. I could see at once that there was no way through, that the only way was to jump the wire, and when I saw Topthorn and Captain Stewart leap over where the wire was lowest. I followed them and we found ourselves at last in among the enemy. From behind every tree, from trenches all around it seemed, they ran forward in their piked helmets to counterattack. They rushed past us, ignoring us until we found ourselves surrounded by an entire company of soldiers, their rifles pointing up at us.

The crump of the shelling and the spitting of rifle fire had suddenly stopped. I looked around me for the rest of the squadron, to discover that we were alone. Behind us the riderless horses, all that was left of a proud cavalry squadron, galloped back toward our trenches, and the hillside below was strewn with the dead and dying.

"Throw down your sword, Trooper," said Captain Stewart, bending in his saddle and dropping his sword to the ground. "There's been enough useless slaughter today.

No sense in adding to it." He walked Topthorn closer toward us and reined in. "Trooper, I told you once we had the best horses in the squadron, and today they showed us they are the best horses in the entire regiment, in the whole confounded army – and there's not a scratch on them." He dismounted as the German soldiers closed in and Trooper Warren followed suit. They stood side by side holding our reins while we were surrounded. We looked back down the hill at the battlefield. A few horses were still struggling on the wire, but one by one they were put out of their misery by the advancing German infantry, who had already regained their line of trenches. They were the last shots in the battle.

"What a waste," the captain said. "What a ghastly waste. Maybe now when they see this they'll understand that you can't send horses into wire and machine guns. Maybe now they'll think again."

The soldiers around us seemed wary of us and kept their distance. They seemed not to know quite what to do with us. "The horses, sir?" Trooper Warren asked. "Joey and Topthorn, what happens to them now?"

"Same as us, Trooper," said Captain Stewart. "They're prisoners of war just as we are." Flanked by the soldiers who hardly spoke, we were escorted over the brow of a hill and down into the valley below. Here the valley was still green for there had been no battle over this ground as yet. All the while, Trooper Warren had his arm over my neck to reassure me, and I felt then that he was beginning to say good-bye.

He spoke softly into my ear. "Don't suppose they'll let you come with me where I'm going, Joey. I wish they could, but they can't. But I shan't ever forget you. I promise you that."

"Don't you worry, Trooper," Captain Stewart said. "The Germans love their horses every bit as much as we do. They'll be all right. Anyway, Topthorn will look after your Joey — you can be sure of that."

As we came out of the woods and onto the road below, we were halted by our escort. Captain Stewart and Trooper Warren were marched away down the road toward a cluster of ruined buildings that must at one time have been a village, while Topthorn and I were led away across the fields and farther down the valley. There was no time for long farewells — just a brief last stroke of the muzzle for each of us and they were gone. As they walked away, Captain Stewart had his arm around Trooper Warren's shoulder.

CHAPTER 9

W E WERE LED AWAY BY TWO NERVOUS SOLDIERS down farm tracks, through orchards, and across a bridge before being tied up beside a hospital tent some miles from where we had been captured. A knot of wounded soldiers gathered around us at once. They patted and stroked us, and I began to whisk my tail with impatience. I was hungry and thirsty and angry that I had been separated from my Trooper Warren.

Still no one seemed to know quite what to do with us until an officer in a long gray coat with a bandage around his head emerged from the tent. He was an immensely tall man standing a full head higher than anyone around him. The manner of his gait and the way he held himself indicated a man clearly accustomed to wielding authority. A bandage came down over one eye so that he had only half a face visible. As he walked toward us I saw that he was limping, that one foot was heavily bandaged and that he needed the support of a stick. The soldiers sprang back at his approach and stood stiffly to attention. He looked us both over in undisguised admiration, shaking his head and sighing as he did so. Then he turned to the men. "There are hundreds like these dead out on our wire. I tell you, if we had had one jot of the courage of these animals, we would be in Paris by now and not slugging it out here in the mud. These two horses came through hellfire to get here – they were the only two to make it. It was not their fault they were sent on a fool's errand. They are not circus animals, they are heroes – do you understand, heroes – and they should be treated as such. And you stand around and gawk at them. None of you are badly wounded, and the doctor is far too busy to see you at present. So, I want these horses unsaddled, rubbed down, fed, and watered at once. They will need oats and hay, and a blanket for each of them, now get moving."

The soldiers hurried away, scattering in all directions, and within a few minutes, Topthorn and I were being lavished with all manner of clumsy kindness. None of them had handled a horse before, it seemed, but that did not matter to us, so grateful were we for all the food they brought us and the water. We lacked for nothing that morning, and all the time the tall officer supervised from under the trees, leaning on his stick. From time to time he would come up to us and run his hand along our backs and over our quarters, nodding his approval and lecturing his men on the finer points of horse breeding as he examined us. After a time he was joined by a man in a white coat who emerged from the tent, his hair disheveled, his face pale with exhaustion. There was blood on his coat.

"Headquarters phoned through about the horses, Herr Hauptmann," said the man in white. "And they say I am to keep them for the stretcher cases. I know your view on the matter, Hauptmann, but I'm afraid you cannot have them. We need them here desperately, and the way things are going, I fear we will need more. That was just the first attack – there will be more to come. We expect a sustained offensive – it will be a long battle. We are the same on both sides: once we start something, we seem to have to prove a point, and that takes time and lives. We'll need all the ambulance transport we can get, motorized or horse."

The tall officer drew himself up to his full height and bristled with indignation. He was a formidable sight as he advanced on the man in white. "Doctor, you cannot put fine British cavalry horses to pulling carts! Any of our horse regiments – my own Regiment of Lancers would be proud, indeed, overwhelmed to have such splendid creatures in their ranks. You cannot do it, Doctor, I will not permit it."

"Herr Hauptmann," said the doctor patiently – he was clearly not at all intimidated – "do you really imagine, after this morning's madness, that either side will be using cavalry again in this war? Can you not understand that we need transport, Herr Hauptmann? And we need it now. There are men, brave men, German and English, lying out there on stretchers in the trenches, and at present there's not enough transport to bring them back to the hospital here. Now, do you want them all to die, Herr Hauptmann? Tell me that. Do you want them to die? If these horses could be hitched up to a cart, they could bring them back in dozens. We just do not have enough ambulances to cope, and what we do have break down or get stuck in the mud. Please, Herr Hauptmann. We need your help."

"The world," said the German officer, shaking his head, "the world has gone quite mad. When noble creatures such as these are forced to become beasts of burden, the world has gone mad. But I can see that you are right. I am a lancer, Herr Doctor, but even I know that men are more important than horses. But you must see to it that you have someone in charge of these two who knows horses – I don't want any dirty-fingered mechanic getting his hand on these two. And you must tell them that they are riding horses. They won't take kindly to pulling carts, no matter how noble the cause."

"Thank you, Herr Hauptmann," said the doctor. "You are most kind, but I have a problem, Herr Hauptmann. As I am sure you will agree, they will need an expert to manage them to start with, particularly if they have never been put in a cart before. The problem is that I have only medical orderlies here. True, one of them has worked horses on a farm before the war, but to tell you the truth, Herr Hauptmann, I have no one who could manage these two – no one, that is, except you. You are due to go to the base hospital on the next convoy of ambulances, but they won't be here before this evening. I know it's a lot to ask of a wounded man, but you can see how desperate I am. The farmer down below has several carts, and I should imagine all the harnesses you would need. What do you say, Herr Hauptmann? Can you help me?"

The bandaged officer limped back toward us and stroked our noses tenderly. Then he smiled and nodded. "Very well. It's a sacrilege, Doctor, a sacrilege," he said. "But if it's got to be done, then I'd rather do it myself and see that it is done properly."

So that same afternoon after our capture, Topthorn and

I were hitched up side by side to an old hay cart and with the officer directing two orderlies, we were driven up through the woods, back toward the thunder of the gunfire and the wounded that awaited us. Topthorn was all the time in a great state of alarm, for it was clear he had never pulled before in his life, and at last I was able in my turn to help him, to lead, to compensate, and to reassure him. The officer led us at first, limping along beside me with his stick, but he was soon confident enough to mount the cart with the two orderlies and take the reins. "You've done a bit of this before, my friend," he said. "I can tell that. I always knew the British were crazy. Now that I know that they use horses such as you as cart horses, I am quite sure of it. That's what this war is all about, my friend. It's about which of us is the crazier. And clearly you British started with an advantage. You were crazy beforehand."

All that afternoon and evening while the battle raged, we trudged up to the lines, loaded up with the stretchers, and brought them back to the field hospital. It was several miles each way over roads and tracks filled with shell holes and littered with the corpses of mules and men. The artillery barrage from both sides was continuous. It roared overhead all day as the armies hurled their men at one another across no-man's-land, and the wounded that could walk poured back along the roads. I had seen the same gray faces looking out from under their helmets somewhere before. All that was different were the uniforms – they were gray now with red piping, and the helmets were no longer round with a broad brim.

It was almost night before the tall officer left us, waving good-bye to us and to the doctor from the back of the ambulance as it bumped its way across the field and out of sight. The doctor turned to the orderlies who had been with us all day. "See to it that they are well cared for, those two," he said. "They saved good lives today, those two – good German lives and good English lives. They deserve the best of care. See to it that they have it."

For the first time that night since we came to the war, Topthorn and I had the luxury of a stable. The shed in the farm that lay across the fields from the hospital was emptied of pigs and poultry, and we were led in to find a rack brimming full with sweet hay and buckets of soothing, cold water.

That night after we had finished our hay, Topthorn and I were lying down together at the back of the shed. I was half awake and could think only of my aching muscles and sore feet. Suddenly the door creaked open and the stable was filled with a flickering orange light. Behind the light there were footsteps. We looked up and I was seized at that moment with a kind of panic. For a fleeting moment I imagined myself back at home in the stable with old Zoey. The dancing light triggered off an alarm in me, reminding me at once of Albert's father. I was on my feet in an instant and backing away from the light with Topthorn beside me, protecting me. However, when the voice spoke, it was not the rasping, drunken voice of Albert's father, but rather a soft, gentle tone of a girl's voice, a young girl. I could see now that there were two people behind the light: an old man, a bent old man in rough clothes and clogs, and beside him stood a young girl, her head and shoulders wrapped in a shawl.

"There you are, Grandpapa," she said. "I told you they put them in here. Have you ever seen anything so beautiful? Oh, can they be mine, Grandpapa? Please, can they be mine?"

CHAPTER 10

I
F IT IS POSSIBLE TO BE HAPPY IN THE MIDDLE OF A NIGHT-
mare, then Topthorn and I were happy that summer.
Every day we had to make the same hazardous journeys
up to the front line, which, in spite of almost continuous
offensives and counteroffensives, moved only a matter of a
few hundred yards in either direction. Hauling our ambulance cart of dying and wounded back from the trenches,
we became a familiar sight along the pitted track. More than
once we were cheered by marching soldiers as they passed
us. Once, after we had plodded on, too tired to be fearful,
through a devastating barrage that straddled the road in
front of us and behind us, one of the soldiers with his tunic
covered in blood and mud, came and stood by my head and
threw his good arm around my neck and kissed me.

"Thank you, my friend," he said. "I never thought they
would get us out of that hellhole. I found this yesterday,

and thought about keeping it for myself, but I know where it belongs." And he reached up and hung a muddied ribbon around my neck. There was an Iron Cross dangling on the end of it. "You'll have to share it with your friend," he said. "They tell me you're both English. I bet you are the first English in this war to win an Iron Cross, and the last I shouldn't wonder." The waiting wounded outside the hospital tent clapped and cheered us to the echo, bringing doctors, nurses, and patients running out of the tent to see what there could be to clap about in the midst of all this misery.

They hung our Iron Cross on a nail outside our stable door and on the rare quiet days, when the shelling stopped and we were not needed to make the journey up to the front, a few of the walking wounded would wander down from the hospital to the farmyard to visit us. I was puzzled by this adulation but loved it, thrusting my head over the high stable door whenever I heard them coming into the yard. Side by side, Topthorn and I would stand at the door to receive our unlimited ration of compliments and adoration – and, of course, this was sometimes accompanied by a welcome gift of perhaps a lump of sugar or an apple.

But it is the evenings of that summer that stay so strong in my memory. Often it would not be until dusk that we would clatter into the yard, and there, always waiting by the stable door, would be the little girl and her grandfather who had come to us that first evening. The orderlies simply handed us over into their charge – and that was just as well, for kind as they were, they had no notion about horses. It was little Emilie and her grandfather who insisted that they should look after us. They rubbed us down and saw to our sores and bruises. They fed us, watered us, and groomed us and somehow always found enough straw for a dry warm bed. Emilie made us each a fringe to tie over our eyes to keep the flies from bothering us, and in the warm summer evenings she led us out to graze in the meadow below the farmhouse and stayed with us watching us grazing until her grandfather called us in again.

She was a tiny, frail creature, but led us about the farm with complete confidence, chatting all the while about what she had been doing all the day and about how brave we were and how proud she was of us.

As winter came on again and the grass lost its flavor and goodness, she would climb up into the loft above the stable and throw down our hay for us, and she would lie down on the loft floor looking at us through the trapdoor while we pulled the hay from the rack and ate it. Then, with her grandfather busying himself about us, she would prattle on merrily about how when she was older and stronger and when the soldiers had all gone home and the war was over she would ride us herself through the woods – one at a time, she said – and how we would never want for anything if only we would stay with her forever.

Topthorn and I were by now seasoned campaigners, and it may well have been that that drove us on out through the roar of the shell fire back toward the trenches each morning, but there was more to it than that. For us it was the hope that we would be back that evening in our stable and that little Emilie would be there to comfort and to love us. We had that to look forward to and to long for. Any horse has an instinctive fondness for children, for they speak more softly, and their size precludes any threat; but Emilie was a special child for us, for she spent every minute she could with us and lavished us with her affection. She would be up late every evening with us, rubbing us down and seeing to our feet, and be up again at dawn to see us fed properly before the orderlies led us away and hitched us up to the ambulance cart. She would climb the wall by the pond and stand there waving, and although I could never turn around, I knew she would stay there until the road took us out of sight. And then she would be there when we came back in the evening, clasping her hands in excitement as she watched us being unhitched.

But one evening at the onset of winter, she was not there to greet us. We had been worked even harder that day than usual, for the first snows of winter had blocked the road up to the trenches to all but the horse-drawn vehicles and we had to make twice the number of trips to bring in the wounded. Exhausted, hungry, and thirsty, we were led into our stable by Emilie's grandfather, who said not a word but saw to us quickly before hurrying back across the yard to the house. Topthorn and I spent that evening by the stable door watching the gentle fall of snow and the flickering light in the farmhouse. We knew something was wrong before the old man came back and told us.

He came late at night, his feet crumping the snow. He had made up the buckets of hot mash we had come to expect and he sat down on the straw beneath the lantern and watched us eat. "She prays for you," he said, nodding slowly. "Do you know, every night before she goes to bed, she prays for you? I've heard her. She prays for her dead father and mother — they were killed only a week after the war began. One shell, that's all it takes. And she prays for her brother that she'll never see again — just seventeen and he doesn't even have a grave. It's as if he never lived except in our minds. Then she prays for me and for the war to pass by the farm and to leave us alone, and last of all she prays for you two. She prays for two things: first, that you both survive the war and live on into ripe old age, and secondly, that if you do she dearly wants to be there to be with you. She's barely thirteen, my Emilie, and now she's lying up there in her room and I don't know if she'll live to see the morning. The German doctor from the hospital tells me it's pneumonia. He's a good enough doctor even if he is German – he's done his best, it's up to God now, and so far God hasn't done too well for my family. If she goes, if my Emilie dies, then the only light left in my life will be put out." He looked up at us through heavily wrinkled eyes and wiped the tears from his face. "If you can understand anything of what I said, then pray for her to whatever horse god you pray to – pray for her like she does for you."

There was heavy shelling all that night, and before dawn the next day, the orderlies came for us and led us out into the snow to be hitched up. There was no sign of Emilie nor her grandfather. Pulling the cart through the fresh, uncut snow that morning, Topthorn and I needed all our strength just to haul the empty cart up to the front line. The snow disguised perfectly the ruts and shell holes, so that we found ourselves straining to extricate ourselves from the piled-up snow and the sinking mud beneath it.

We made it to the front line, but only with the help of

the two orderlies, who jumped out whenever we had difficulty and turned the wheels over by hand until we were
free again and the cart could gather momentum through
the snow once more.

The field station behind the front line was crowded with
wounded and we had to bring back a heavier load than
we ever had before, but fortunately the way back was
mostly downhill. Someone suddenly remembered it was
Christmas morning, and they sang slow, tuneful carols all
the way back. For the most part they were casualties blinded
by gas and in their pain some of them cried, as they sang,
for their lost sight. We made so many journeys that day
and stopped only when the hospital could take no more.

It was already a starry night by the time we reached the
farm. The shelling had stopped. There were no flares to
light up the sky and blot out the stars. All the way along
the lane, not a gun fired. Peace had come for one night,
one at least. The snow in the yard was crisped by the frost.
There was a dancing light in our stable, and Emilie's grandfather came out into the snow and took our reins from the
orderly.

"It's a fine night," he said to us as he led us in. "It's a fine
night and all's well. There's mash and hay and water in
there for you — I've given you extra tonight, not because

it's cold, but because you prayed. You must have prayed to that horse god of yours because my Emilie woke up at lunchtime, sat up she did, and do you know the first thing she said? I'll tell you. She said, 'I must get up, got to get their mash ready for them when they come back. They'll be cold and tired,' she said. The only way that German doctor could get her to stay in bed was to promise you extra rations tonight, and she made him promise to go on with them as long as the cold weather lasted. So go inside, my beauties, and eat your fill. We've all had a Christmas present today, haven't we? All's well, I tell you. All's well."

CHAPTER 11

AND ALL WAS TO STAY WELL FOR A TIME AT LEAST, for the war suddenly moved away from us that spring. We knew it was not over because we could still hear distant thunder of the guns, and the troops came marching through the farmyard from time to time up toward the line. But there were fewer wounded now to bring in and we were needed less and less to pull our ambulance cart back and forth from the trenches. Topthorn and I were put out to graze in the meadow by the pond most days, but the evenings were still cold with the occasional frost, and our Emilie would always come to get us in before dark. She did not need to lead us. She only had to call and we followed.

Emilie was still weak from her illness and coughed a great deal as she fussed around us in the stable. From time to time now, she would heave herself up onto my back and I would walk so gently around the yard and out into the meadow with Topthorn following close behind. She used no reins on me, no saddle, no bits, no spurs, and sat astride me not as my mistress, but rather as a friend. Topthorn was just that much taller and broader than me, and she found it very difficult to mount him and even more difficult to get down. Sometimes she would use me as a stepping stone to Topthorn, but it was a difficult maneuver for her, and more than once she fell off in the attempt.

But between Topthorn and me there was never any jealousy, and he was quite content to plod around beside us and take her on board whenever she felt like it. One evening we were out in the meadow, sheltering under the chestnut tree from the heat of the new summer sun, when we heard the sound of an approaching convoy of trucks coming back from the front. As they came through the farm gate, they called out to us and we recognized them as the orderlies, nurses, and doctors from the field hospital. As the convoy stopped in the yard we galloped over to the gate by the pond and looked over. Emilie and her grandfather emerged from the milking shed and were deep in conversation with the doctor. Quite suddenly we found ourselves besieged by all the orderlies we had come to know so well. They climbed the fence and patted and smoothed us with great affection. They were exuberant, yet somehow sad at the same time. Emilie was running over toward us, shouting and screaming.

"I knew it would happen," she said. "I knew it. I prayed for it to happen and it did happen. They don't need you anymore to pull their carts. They're moving the hospital farther up along the valley. There's a big, big battle going on up there and so they're moving away from us. But they don't want to take you with them. That kind doctor has told Grandpapa that you can both stay – it's a kind of payment for the cart they used and the food they took and because we looked after you throughout all the winter. He says you can stay and work on the farm until the army needs you again – and they never will, and if they ever did, I'd hide you. We'll never let them take you away, will we, Grandpapa? Never, never."

And so after the long, sad farewells, the convoy moved away up the road in a cloud of dust and we were left alone and in peace with Emilie and her grandfather. The peace was to prove sweet but short-lived.

To my great delight, I found myself once more a farm horse. With Topthorn harnessed up beside me, we set to work the very next day cutting and turning the hay. When Emilie protested, after that first long day in the fields, that her grandfather was working us too hard, he put his hands on her shoulders and said, "Nonsense, Emilie. They like to work. They need to work. And besides, the only way for us to go on living, Emilie, is to go on like we did before. The soldiers have gone now, so if we pretend hard enough, then maybe the war will go away altogether. We must live as we have always lived, cutting our hay, picking our apples, and tilling our soil. We cannot live as if there will be no tomorrow. We can live only if we eat, and our food comes from the land. We must work the land if we want to live and these two must work it with us. They don't mind — they like the work. Look at them, Emilie — do they look unhappy?"

For Topthorn, the transition from pulling an ambulance cart to pulling a hay turner was not a difficult one, and he adapted easily. And for me, it was a dream I had dreamed many times since I had left the farm in Devon. I was working once more with happy, laughing people around me who cared for me. We pulled with a will that harvest, Topthorn and I, hauling in the heavy hay wagons to the barns where Emilie and her grandfather would unload. And Emilie continued to watch over us lovingly — every scratch and bruise was tended to at once and her grandfather was never allowed to work us for too long, however much he argued. But the return to the peaceful life of a farm horse could not last long, not in the middle of that war.

The hay was almost all gathered in when the soldiers came back again one evening. We were in our stables when we heard the sound of approaching hoofbeats and the rumbling of wheels on the cobblestones as the column came trotting into the yard. The horses, six at a time, were yoked to huge heavy guns, and they stood in the path, puffing and blowing with exertion. Each pair was ridden by men whose faces were severe and hard under their gray caps. I noticed at once that these were not the gentle orderlies that had left us only a few short weeks before. Their faces were strange and harsh and there was a new alarm and urgency in their eyes. Few of them seemed to laugh or even smile. These were a different breed of men from those we had seen before. Only one old soldier who drove the ammunition cart came over to stroke us and spoke kindly to little Emilie.

After a brief consultation with Emilie's grandfather, the artillery troop camped in our meadow that night, watering the horses in our pond. Topthorn and I were excited by the arrival of new horses and spent all evening with our heads over the stable door neighing to them, but most of them seemed too tired to reply. Emilie came to tell us about the soldiers that evening and we could see she was worried, for she would talk only a whisper.

"Grandpapa doesn't like them here," she said. "He doesn't trust the officer, says he's got eyes like a wasp and you can't trust a wasp. But they'll be gone in the morning, then we'll be on our own again."

Early that next morning, as the dark of night left the sky, a visitor came to our stables. It was a pale, thin man in a dusty uniform who peered over the door to inspect us. He had eyes that stood out of his face in a permanent stare, and he wore a pair of wire-framed spectacles through which he watched us intently, nodding as he did so. He stood a few minutes and then left.

By full light the artillery troop was drawn up in the yard and ready to move. There was a loud and incessant knocking on the farmhouse door, and we saw Emilie and her grandfather come out into the yard still dressed in their nightclothes. "Your horses, monsieur," the bespectacled officer announced baldly. "I shall be taking your horses with us. I have one team with only four horses, and I need two more. They look fine, strong animals, and they will learn quickly. We will be taking them with us."

"But how can I work my farm without horses?" Emilie's

grandfather said. "They are just farm horses – they won't be able to pull guns."

"Sir," said the officer, "there is a war on, and I have to have horses for my guns. I have to take them. What you do on your farm is your own business, but I must have the horses. The army needs them."

"But you can't," Emilie cried. "They're my horses. You can't take them. Don't let them, Grandpapa, don't let them, please don't let them."

The old man shrugged his shoulders sadly. "My child," he said quietly, "what can I do? How could I stop them? Do you suggest I cut them to pieces with my scythe or chop them up with my ax? No, my child, we knew it might happen one day, didn't we? We talked about it often enough, didn't we? We knew they would go one day. Now, I want no tears in front of these people. You're to be proud and strong like your brother was, and I'll not have you weaken in front of them. Go and say your good-byes to the horses, Emilie, and be brave."

Little Emilie led us to the back of the stable and slipped our halters on, carefully arranging our manes so that they were not snagged by the rope. Then she reached up and put her arms about us, leaning her head into each of us in turn and crying softly. "Come back," she said. "Please come back to me. I shall die if you don't come back." She wiped her eyes and pushed back her hair before opening the stable door and leading us out into the yard. She walked us directly toward the officer and handed over the reins. "I want them back," she said, her voice strong now, almost fierce. "I'm just lending them to you. They are my horses. They belong here. Feed them well and look after them and make sure you bring them back." And she walked past her grandfather and into the house without even turning around.

As we left the farm, hauled unwillingly along behind the ammunition cart, I turned and saw Emilie's grandfather still standing in the yard. He was smiling and waving at us through his tears. Then the rope jerked my neck violently around and jolted me into a trot, and I recalled the time once before when I had been roped up to a cart and dragged away against my will. But at least this time I had my Topthorn with me.

CHAPTER 12

ERHAPS IT WAS THE CONTRAST WITH THE FEW IDYLLIC months we had spent with Emilie and her grandfather that made what followed so harsh and so bitter an experience for Topthorn and me. Or perhaps it was just that the war was all the time becoming more terrible. In places, the guns were now lined up only a few yards apart for miles and miles, and when they sounded out their fury, the very earth shook beneath us. The lines of wounded seemed interminable, and the countryside was laid waste for miles behind the trenches.

The work itself was certainly no harder than when we had been pulling the ambulance cart, but now we were no longer stabled every night, and of course we no longer had the protection of our Emilie to rely on. Suddenly the war was no longer distant. We were back among the fearful noise and stench of battle, hauling our gun through the mud, urged on and sometimes whipped on by men who displayed little care or interest in our welfare just so long as we got the guns where they had to go. It was not that they were cruel men, but just that they seemed to be driven now by a fearful compulsion that left no room and no time for pleasantness or consideration either for each other or for us.

Food was scarcer now. We received our corn ration only sporadically as winter came on again, and there was only a meager hay ration for each of us. One by one, we began to lose weight and condition. At the same time, the battles seemed to become more furious and prolonged, and we worked longer and harder hours pulling in front of the gun; we were permanently sore and permanently cold. We ended every day covered in a layer of cold, dripping mud that seemed to seep through and chill us to the bones.

The gun team was a motley collection of six horses. Of the four we joined, only one had the height and the strength to pull as a gun horse should, a great hulk of a horse they called Heinie who seemed quite unperturbed by all that was going on around him. The rest of the team tried to live up to his example, but only Topthorn succeeded. Heinie and Topthorn were the leading pair, and I found myself in the ruts behind Topthorn next to a thin, wiry little horse they called Coco. He had a display of white patch marks over his face that often caused amusement among the soldiers as we passed by. But there was nothing funny about Coco — he had the nastiest temper of any horse I had ever met, either before or since. When Coco was eating, no one — neither horse nor man — ventured within biting or kicking distance. Behind us was a perfectly matched pair of smaller dun-colored ponies with blond manes and tails. No one could tell them apart, even the soldiers referred to them not by name but merely as "the two golden Haflingers." Because they were pretty and invariably friendly, they received much attention and even a little affection from the gunners. They must have been an incongruous but cheering sight to the tired soldiers as we trotted through the ruined villages up to the front. There was no doubt that they worked as hard as the rest of us and that, in spite of their diminutive size, they were at least our equals in stamina. But in a canter they acted as a brake, slowed us down, and spoiled the rhythm of the team.

Strangely enough, it was the giant Heinie who showed the first signs of weakness. The cold, sinking mud and the lack of proper food through that appalling winter began to shrink his massive frame and reduced him within months to a poor, skinny-looking creature. So to my delight — and I must confess it — they moved me up into the leading pair with Topthorn, and Heinie dropped back now to pull alongside little Coco, who had begun the ordeal with little strength in reserve. They both went rapidly downhill until the two of them were only any use for pulling on flat, hard surfaces, and since we scarcely ever traveled over such ground, they were soon of little use in the team, and made the work for the rest of us that much more arduous.

Each night we spent in the lines up to our hocks in freezing mud, in conditions far worse than that first winter of the war when Topthorn and I had been cavalry horses. Then each horse had had a trooper who did all he could to care for us and comfort us, but now the efficiency of the gun was the first priority and we came in a very poor second. We were mere workhorses, and treated as such. The gunners themselves were gray in the face with exhaustion and hunger. Survival was all that mattered to them now. Only the kind old gunner I had noticed that first day when we were taken from the farm seemed to have the time to stay with us. He fed us with hard bits of crumbly black bread and spent more time with us than with his fellow soldiers, whom he seemed to avoid all he could. He was an untidy, portly little man who chuckled incessantly and would talk more to himself than to anyone else.

The effects of continual exposure, underfeeding, and

hard work were now apparent in all of us. Few of us had any hair growing on our lower legs and the skin below was a mass of cracked sores. Even the rugged little Haflingers began to lose weight and muscle. Like all the others, I found every step I took now excruciatingly painful, particularly in my forelegs, which were cracking badly from the knees downward, and there was not a horse in the team that was not walking lame. The vets treated us as best they could, and even the most hard-hearted of the gunners seemed disturbed as our condition worsened, but there was nothing anyone could do until the mud disappeared.

The field vets shook their heads in despair and pulled back those they could for rest and recuperation, but some had deteriorated so much that they were led away and shot there and then after the vet's inspection. Heinie went that way one morning, and we passed him lying in the mud, a collapsed wreck of a horse, and so eventually did Coco, who was hit in his neck by flying shrapnel and had to be destroyed where he lay by the side of the road. No matter how much I disliked him — and he was a vicious beast — it was a piteous and terrible sight to see a fellow creature, with whom I had pulled for so long, discarded and forgotten in a ditch.

The little Haflingers stayed with us all through the winter, straining their broad backs and pulling against the ruts with all the strength they could muster. They were both gentle and kind, with not a shred of aggression in their courageous souls, and Topthorn and I came to love them dearly. In their turn, they looked up to us for support and friendship, and we gave both willingly.

I first noticed that Topthorn was failing when I felt the gun pulling more heavily than before. We were fording a small stream when the wheels of the gun became stuck in the mud. I turned quickly to look at him and saw him suddenly laboring and low in his stride. His eyes told me the pain he was suffering, and I pulled all the harder to enable him to ease up.

That night, with the rain sheeting down relentlessly on our backs, I stood over him as he lay down in the mud. He lay not on his stomach as he always did, but stretched out on his side, lifting his head from time to time as spasms of coughing shook him. He coughed intermittently all night and slept only fitfully. I worried over him, nuzzling him and licking him to try to keep him warm and to reassure him that he was not alone in his pain. I consoled myself with the thought that no horse I had ever seen had the power and stamina of Topthorn, and that he must have a reservoir of great strength to fall back on in his sickness.

And sure enough, he was up on his feet the next morning before the gunners came to feed us our ration of corn, and although his head hung lower than usual and he moved only ponderously, I could see that he had the strength to survive if only he could rest.

I noticed, however, that when the vet came that day checking along the lines, he looked long and hard at Topthorn and listened carefully to his chest. "He's a strong one," I heard him tell the spectacled officer – a man whom no one liked, neither horses nor men. "There's fine breeding here – too fine, perhaps, Herr Major. Could well be his undoing. He's too fine to pull a gun. I'd pull him out, but you have no horse to take his place, have you? He'll go on, I suppose, but go easy on him, Herr Major. Take the team as slow as you can, else you'll have no team, and without your team your gun won't be a lot of use, will it?"

"He will have to do what the others do, Herr Doctor," said the major in a steely voice. "No more and no less. I cannot make exceptions. If you pass him fit, he's fit and that's that."

"He's fit to go on," said the vet reluctantly. "But I am warning you, Herr Major. You must take care."

"We do what we can," said the major dismissively. And, to be fair, they did. It was the mud that was killing us one by one – the mud, the lack of shelter, and the lack of food.

CHAPTER 13

S
O TOPTHORN CAME INTO THAT SPRING WEAKENED
severely by his illness and still with a husky cough,
but he had survived. We had both survived. There
was hard ground to go on now, and the grass grew once
more in the fields so that our bodies began to fill out
again, and our coats lost their winter raggedness and
shone in the sun. The sun shone also on the soldiers,
whose uniforms of gray and red stayed cleaner. They
shaved more often now, and they began as they always
did every spring to talk of the end of the war and about
home and about how the next attack would finish
it and how they would see their families again soon. They
were happier, and so they treated us that much better.
The rations improved, too, with the weather, and our gun
team stepped out with a new enthusiasm and purpose.
The sores disappeared from our legs and we had full

bellies each day, all the grass we could eat, and plenty of oats.

The two little Haflingers puffed and snorted behind us, and they shamed Topthorn and me into a gallop – something we had not been able to achieve all winter no matter how hard our riders tried to whip us on. Our newfound health and the optimism of the singing, whistling soldiers brought us to a fresh sense of exhilaration as we rolled our guns along the pitted roads into position.

But there were to be no battles for us that summer. There was always a sporadic firing and shelling, but the armies seemed content to growl at each other and threaten without ever coming to grips. Farther away, of course, we heard the renewed fury of the spring offensive up and down the line, but we were not needed to move our guns and spent that summer in comparative peace some way behind the lines. Idleness – even boredom – set in as we grazed the lush buttercup meadows and we even became fat for the first time since we came to war. Perhaps it was because we became too fat that Topthorn and I were chosen to pull the ammunition cart from the railroad some miles away up to the artillery lines, and so we found ourselves under the command of the kind old soldier who had been so good to us all winter.

Everyone called him Crazy Old Friedrich. He was

thought to be crazy because he talked continuously to himself, and even when he was not talking, he was laughing and chortling at some private joke that he never shared with anyone. Crazy Old Friedrich was the old soldier they set to work on tasks no one else wanted to do because he was always obliging and everyone knew it.

In the heat and the dust it was tedious and strenuous work that quickly took off our excess weight and began to sap our strength once more. The cart was always too heavy for us to pull because they insisted at the railroad on filling it up with as many shells as possible in spite of Friedrich's protestations. They simply laughed at him, ignored him, and piled on the shells. On the way back to the artillery lines Friedrich would always walk up the hills, leading us slowly for he knew how heavy the wagon must have been. We stopped often for rests and for water, and he made quite sure that we had more food than the other horses who were resting all that summer.

We came to look forward now to each morning when Friedrich would come to fetch us in from the field and put on our harness and we would leave the noise and the bustle of the camp behind us. We soon discovered that Friedrich was not in the slightest bit crazy, but simply a kind and gentle man whose whole nature cried out against fighting a war. He confessed to us, as we plodded along the road to the railroad, that he longed only to be back in his butcher's shop in Schleiden, and that he talked to himself because he felt that he was the only one who understood himself or would even listen to what he was saying. He laughed to himself, he said, because if he did not laugh he would cry.

"I tell you, my friends," he said one day, "I tell you that I am the only sane man in the regiment. It's the others who are crazy, but they don't know it. They fight a war and they don't know what for. Isn't that crazy? How can one man kill another and not really know the reason why he does it, except that the other man wears a different color uniform and speaks a different language? And it's me they call crazy! You two are the only rational creatures I've met in this stupid war, and like me, the only reason you're here is because you were brought here. If I had the courage — and I haven't — we'd take off down this road and never come back. But then they'd shoot me when they caught me, and my wife and my children and my mother and my father would have the shame of it on them forever. As it is, I'm going to live out this war as 'Crazy Old Friedrich,' so that I can return again to Schleiden and become Butcher Friedrich that everyone knew and respected before all this mess began."

As the weeks passed, it became apparent that Friedrich

took a particular liking to Topthorn. Knowing he had been ill, he took more time and care over him, attending to the slightest sore before it could develop and make life uncomfortable for Topthorn. He was kind to me as well, but I think he never had the same affection for me. It was noticeable that he would often stand back and simply gaze at Topthorn with love and glowing admiration in his eyes. There seemed to be an empathy between them, that of one soldier to another.

The summer passed slowly into autumn, and it became clear that our time with Friedrich was coming to an end. Such was Friedrich's attachment to Topthorn by now that he volunteered to ride him out on the gun-team exercises that were to precede the autumn campaign. Of course, all the gunners laughed at the suggestion, but they were always short of good horsemen – and no one denied he was that – and so we found ourselves the leading pair once again with Crazy Old Friedrich riding on Topthorn. We had found at last a true friend and one we could trust implicitly.

"If I have to die out here away from my home," Friedrich confided to Topthorn one day, "I would rather die alongside you. But I'll do my best to see to it that we all get through and get back home – that much I promise you."

CHAPTER 14

S
O FRIEDRICH RODE WITH US THAT AUTUMN DAY WHEN
we went to war again. The gun troop was resting at
midday under the welcome shade of a large chestnut woods that covered both banks of a silver, glinting
river that was full of splashing, laughing men. As we
moved in among the trees and the guns were unhitched, I
saw that the entire woods were crowded with resting soldiers, their helmets, packs, and rifles lying beside them.
They sat back against the trees smoking, or lay out flat on
their backs and slept.

As we had come to expect, a crowd of them soon came
over to fondle the two golden Haflingers, but one young
soldier approached Topthorn and stood looking up at him,
his face full of open admiration. "Now there's a horse," he
said, calling his friend over. "Come and look at this one,
Karl. Have you ever seen a finer-looking animal? He has

the head of an Arabian. You can see the speed of an English Thoroughbred in his legs and the strength of a Hanoverian in his back and in his neck. He has the best of everything." He reached up and gently rubbed his fist against Topthorn's nose.

"Don't you ever think about anything else except horses, Rudi?" said his companion, keeping his distance. "Three years I've known you and not a day goes by without you going on about the wretched creatures. I know you were brought up with them on your farm, but I still can't understand what it is that you see in them. They are just four legs, a head, and a tail, all controlled by a very little brain that can't think beyond food and drink."

"How can you say that?" said Rudi. "Just look at him, Karl. Can you not see that he's something special? This one isn't just any old horse. There's a nobility in his eye, a regal serenity about him. Does he not personify all that men try to be and never can be? I tell you, my friend, there's divinity in a horse, and especially in a horse like this. God got it right the day he created them. And to find a horse like this in the middle of this filthy abomination of a war is for me like finding a butterfly on a dung heap. We don't belong in the same universe with a creature like this."

To me the soldiers had appeared to become younger as

the war went on, and certainly Rudi was no exception to this. Under his short, cropped hair that was still damp from wearing his helmet, he looked barely the same age as my Albert as I remembered him. And like so many of them now, he looked, without his helmet, like a child dressed up as a soldier.

When Friedrich led us down to the river to drink, Rudi and his friend came with us. Topthorn lowered his head into the water beside me and shook it vigorously as he usually did, showering me all over my face and neck, and bringing me sweet relief from the heat. He drank long and deep and afterward we stood together for a few moments on the riverbank watching the soldiers playing in the water. The hill back up into the woods was steep and rutty, so it was no surprise that Topthorn stumbled once or twice – he had never been as surefooted as I was – but he regained his balance each time and plodded on beside me up the hill. However, I did notice that he was moving rather wearily and sluggishly, that each step as we went up was becoming more and more of an effort for him. His breathing was suddenly short and rasping. Then, as we neared the shade of the trees, Topthorn stumbled to his knees and did not get up again. I stopped for a moment to give him time to get up, but he did not. He lay where he was, breathing heavily, and lifted his head once to look at me. It was an appeal for help – I could see it in his eyes. Then he slumped forward on his face, rolled over and was quite still. His tongue hung from his mouth, and his eyes looked up at me without seeing me. I bent down to nuzzle him, pushing at his neck in a frantic effort to make him move, to make him wake up, but I knew instinctively that he was already dead, that I had lost my best and dearest friend. Friedrich was down on his knees beside him, his ear pressed to Topthorn's chest. He shook his head as he sat back and looked up at the group of men that had by now gathered around us. "He's dead," Friedrich said quietly, and then more angrily, "for God's sake, he's dead." His face was heavy with sadness. "Why?" he said. "Why does this war have to destroy anything and everything that's fine and beautiful?" He covered his eyes with his hands, and Rudi lifted him gently to his feet.

"Nothing you can do, old man," he said. "He's well out of it. Come on." But old Friedrich would not be led away. I turned once more to Topthorn, still licking and nuzzling him where he lay, although I knew and indeed understood by now the finality of death, but in my grief I felt only that I wanted to stay with him to comfort him.

The veterinary officer attached to the troop came running down the hill followed by all the officers and men in the troop who had just heard what had happened. After a brief inspection he, too, pronounced Topthorn to be dead. "I thought so. I told you so," he said almost to himself. "They can't do it. I see it all the time. Too much work on short rations and living outside all winter. I see it all the time. A horse like this can only stand so much. Heart failure, poor fellow. It makes me angry every time it happens. We should not treat horses like this – we treat our machines better."

"He was a friend," said Friedrich simply, kneeling down again over Topthorn and removing his headcollar. The soldiers stood all around us in complete silence, looking down at the prostrate form of Topthorn, in a moment of spontaneous respect and sadness. Perhaps it was because they had known him for a long time and he had in some way become part of their lives.

As we stood silent on the hillside, I heard the first whistle of a shell above us and saw the first explosion as the shell landed in the river. Suddenly the woods were alive with shouting, rushing soldiers, and the shells were falling around us everywhere. The men in the river, half naked and screaming, ran up into the trees and the shelling seemed to follow them. Trees crashed to the ground and horses and men came running out of the woods in the direction of the ridge above us.

My first inclination was to run with them, to run anywhere to escape the shelling, but Topthorn lay dead at my feet and I would not abandon him. Friedrich, who was holding me now, tried all he could to drag me away up behind the shoulder of the hill, shouting and screaming at me to come if I wanted to live, but no man can move a horse that does not wish to be moved, and I did not want to go. As the shelling intensified and he found himself more and more isolated from his friends as they swarmed away up the hill and out of sight, he threw down my reins and tried to make his escape. But he was too slow, and he had left it too late. He never reached the woods. He was struck down only a few paces from Topthorn, rolled back down the hill, and lay still beside him. The last I saw of my troop were the bobbing blond manes of the two little Haflingers as they struggled to pull the gun up through the trees with the gunners hauling frantically on their reins and straining to push the gun from behind.

CHAPTER 15

I STOOD BY TOPTHORN AND FRIEDRICH ALL THAT DAY AND into the night, leaving them only once to drink briefly at the river. The shelling moved back and forth along the valley, showering grass and earth and trees into the air and leaving behind great craters that smoked as if the earth itself were on fire. But any fear I might have had was overwhelmed by a powerful sense of sadness and love that compelled me to stay with Topthorn for as long as I could. I knew that once I left him I would be alone in the world again, that I would no longer have his strength and support beside me. So I stayed with him and waited.

I remember it was near first light and I was cropping the grass close to where they lay, when I heard through the crump and whistle of the shells the whining sound of motors, accompanied by a terrifying rattle of steel that set my ears back against my head. It came from over the ridge from the direction in which the soldiers had disappeared, a grating, roaring sound that came ever nearer by the minute, and louder again as the shelling died away completely.

Although at the time I did not know it as such, the first tank I ever saw came over the rise of the hill with the cold light of dawn behind it, a great gray lumbering monster that belched out smoke from behind as it rocked down the hillside toward me. I hesitated only for a few moments before blind terror tore me at last from Topthorn's side and sent me bolting down the hill toward the river. I crashed into the river without even knowing whether I should find my feet or not and was halfway up the wooded hill on the other side before I dared stop and turn to see if it was still chasing me. I should never have looked, for the one monster had become several monsters, and they were rolling inexorably down toward me, already past the place where Topthorn lay with Friedrich on the shattered hillside. I waited, secure, I thought, in the shelter of the trees and watched the tanks ford the river before I turned once more to run.

I ran I knew not where. I ran till I could no longer hear that dreadful rattle and until the guns seemed far away. I remember crossing a river again, galloping through empty farmyards, jumping fences and ditches and abandoned trenches, and clattering through deserted, ruined villages before I found myself grazing that evening in a lush, wet meadow and drinking from a clear, pebbly brook. And then exhaustion finally overtook me, sapped the strength from my legs, and forced me to lie down and sleep.

When I woke, it was dark and the guns were firing once more all around me. No matter where I looked, it seemed, the sky was lit with the yellow flashes of gunfire and intermittent white glowing lights that pained my eyes and showered daylight briefly onto the countryside around me. Whichever way I went, it seemed, it had to be toward the guns. Better, therefore, I thought, to stay where I was. Here, at least, I had grass in plenty and water to drink.

I had made up my mind to do just that when there was an explosion of white light above my head and the rattle of a machine gun split the night air, the bullets whipping into the ground beside me. I ran again and kept running into the night, stumbling frequently in the ditches and hedges until the fields lost their grass and the trees were mere stumps against the flashing skyline. Wherever I went now, there were great craters in the ground filled with murky, stagnant water.

It was as I staggered out of one such crater that I lumbered into an invisible coil of barbed wire that first snagged and then trapped my foreleg. As I kicked out wildly to free myself, I felt the barbs tearing into my foreleg before I broke clear. From then on I could manage only to limp slowly into the night, feeling my way forward. Even so I must have walked for miles, but where to and where from I shall never know. All the while my leg pulsated with pain, and on every side of me the great guns were sounding out and rifle fire spat into the night. Bleeding, bruised, and terrified beyond belief, I longed only to be with Topthorn again. *He would know which way to go,* I told myself. *He would know.*

I stumbled on into the night, guided only by the belief that where the night was at its blackest, there alone I might find some safety from the shelling. Behind me, the thunder and lightning of the bombardment was so terrible in its intensity, turning the deep black of night into unnatural day, that I could not contemplate going back even though I knew that it was in the direction that Topthorn lay. There was some gunfire ahead of me and on both sides of me, but I could see away in the distance a black horizon of undisturbed night and so moved on steadily toward it.

My wounded leg was stiffening up all the time in the cold of the night, and it pained me now even to lift it. Very soon I found I could put no weight on it at all. This was to be the longest night of my life, a nightmare of agony, terror, and loneliness. I suppose it was only a strong instinct to survive that compelled me to walk on and kept me on my feet. I sensed that my only chance lay in putting the noise of the battle as far behind me as possible, so I had to keep moving. From time to time, rifle fire and machine-gun fire would crackle all around me, and I would stand paralyzed with fear, terrified to move in any direction until the firing stopped and I found my muscles could move once more.

To begin with, I found the mists hovering only in the depths of the craters I passed, but after some hours, I found myself increasingly surrounded in a thick, smoky, autumnal mist through which I could see only the vague shades and shapes of dark and light around me. Almost blinded now, I relied totally on the ever-more-distant roar and rumble of the bombardment, keeping it all the time behind me and moving toward the darker, more silent world ahead of me.

Dawn was already brightening the gloom of the mist when I heard the sound of hushed, urgent voices ahead of me. I stood quite still and listened, straining my eyes to find the people to whom they belonged. "Stand up, get a move on. Get a move on, boys." The voices were muffled in the mist. There was a sound of rushing feet and clattering rifles. "Pick it up, boy, pick it up. What do you think you're doing? Now, clean that rifle off and do it quick." A long silence followed and I moved gingerly toward the voices, both tempted and terrified at the same time.

"There it is again, Sarge. I saw something, honest I did."

"What was it, then, son? The whole German army, or just one or two of them out for a morning stroll?"

"Wasn't a man, Sarge, not even a German, neither – looked more like a horse or cow to me."

"A cow or a horse? Out there in no-man's-land? And how the blazes d'you think it got there? Son, you've been staying up too late – your eyes are playing tricks on you."

"I heard it, too, Sarge, an' all. Honest, Sarge, cross my heart."

"Well, I can't see nothing. I can't see nothing, son, and that's because there's nothing there. You're all of a jitter, son, and your jittering has woke the whole battalion up a half-hour early, and who's going to be a popular little boy when I tell the lieutenant all about it? Spoiled his beauty sleep, haven't you, son? You've gone and woken up all them lovely captains and majors and brigadiers, and all them nice sergeants an' all, just because you thought you'd seen a horse." And then in a louder voice that was intended to carry farther, "But seeing as how we're all awake and there's a pea-soup London smog out there, and seeing as how the Germans like to come a-knocking on our little dugouts just when we can't see them a-coming, I want you boys to keep your eyes peeled back and wide open – then we'll all live to eat our breakfasts, if it's on this morning. There'll be a rum ration coming around in a few minutes – that'll warm you up – but until then I want every one of your eyes skinned."

As he spoke, I limped away. I could feel myself shaking from head to tail in dreadful anticipation of the next bullet or shell, and I wanted only to be alone, away from any noise whatever, whether or not it appeared to be threatening. In my weakened, frightened condition, any sense of reason had left me, and I wandered now through the mists until my good legs could drag me no farther. I stood at last, resting my bleeding leg on a soft, fresh mound of mud beside a foul-smelling, water-filled crater, and I snuffled the ground in vain for something to eat. But the earth where I stood was bare of grass and I had neither the energy nor the will at that moment to move another step forward. I lifted my head again to look about me in case I should discover any grass nearby, and as I did, so I felt the first sunlight filter in through the mist and touch my back sending gentle shivers of warmth through my cold, cramped body.

Within minutes the mist began to clear away and I saw for the first time that I stood in a wide corridor of mud, a wasted, shattered landscape, between two vast, unending rolls of barbed wire that stretched away into the distance behind me and in front of me. I remembered I had been in such a place once before, that day when I had charged across it with Topthorn beside me. This was what the soldiers called "no-man's-land."

CHAPTER 16

FROM BOTH SIDES OF ME I HEARD A GRADUAL CRESCENDO of excitement and laughter rippling along the trenches, interspersed with barked orders that everyone was to keep their heads down and no one was to shoot. From my vantage point on the mound, I could see only an occasional glimpse of a steel helmet, my only evidence that the voices I was hearing did, indeed, belong to real people. There was the sweet smell of cooking food wafting toward me and I lifted my nose to savor it. It was sweeter than the sweetest bran mash I had ever tasted and it had a tinge of salt about it. I was drawn first one way and then the other by this promise of warm food, but each time I neared the trenches on either side, I met an impenetrable barrier of loosely coiled barbed wire. The soldiers cheered me on as I came closer, showing their heads fully now over the trenches and beckoning me toward them, and when I had to turn back at the wire and cross no-man's-land to the other side, I was welcomed again there by a chorus of whistling and clapping, but again I could find no way through the wire. I must have crisscrossed no-man's-land for much of that morning, and found, at long last, in the middle of this blasted wilderness a small patch of coarse, dank grass growing on the lip of an old crater.

I was busying myself at tearing the last of this away when I saw, out of the corner of my eye, a man in a gray uniform climb up out of the trenches, waving a white flag above his head. I looked up as he began to clip his way methodically through the wire and then pull it aside. All this time there was much argument and noisy consternation from the other side, and soon a small, helmeted figure in a flapping khaki overcoat climbed up into no-man's-land. He, too, held up a white handkerchief in one hand and began also to work his way through the wire toward me.

The German was through the wire first, leaving a narrow gap behind him. He approached me slowly across no-man's-land, calling out to me all the while to come toward him. He reminded me at once of dear old Friedrich for he was, like Friedrich, a gray-haired man in an untidy, unbuttoned uniform, and he spoke gently to me. In one hand he held a rope; the other hand he stretched out toward me. He was still far too far away for me to see clearly, but an offered hand in my experience was often cupped and there was enough promise in that for me to limp cautiously toward him. On both sides, the trenches were lined now with cheering men, standing on the walls of the trenches waving their helmets above their heads.

"Oh, boy!" The shout came from behind me and was urgent enough to stop me. I turned to see the small man in khaki weaving quickly his way across no-man's-land, one hand carrying the white handkerchief held high above his head. "Oh, boy! Where you going? Hang on a bit. You're going the wrong way, see."

The two men who were coming toward me could not have been more different. The one in gray was the taller of the two and as he came nearer I could see his face was lined and creased with years. Everything about him was slow and gentle under his ill-fitting uniform. He wore no helmet, but instead the peakless cap with the red band I knew so well sitting carelessly on the back of his head. The little man in khaki reached us, out of breath, his face red and still smooth with youth, his round helmet with the broad rim fallen askew over one ear. For a few strained, silent moments, the two stood yards apart from each other, eyeing one another warily and saying not a word. It was the young man in khaki who broke the silence and spoke first.

"Now what do we do?" he said, walking toward us and looking at the German who stood head and shoulders above him. "There's two of us here and one horse to split between us. 'Course, King Solomon had the answer, didn't he? But it's not very practical in this case, is it? And what's worse, I can't speak a word of German, and I can see you can't understand what the hell I'm talking about, can you? Oh, hell, I should never have come out here, I knew I shouldn't. Can't think what came over me, and all for a muddy old horse, too."

"But I can, I can speak a little bad English," said the older man, still holding out his cupped hand under my nose. It was full of black bread broken into pieces, a tidbit I was familiar enough with but usually found too bitter for my taste. However I was now too hungry to be choosy and as he was speaking I soon emptied his hand. "I speak only a little English – like a schoolboy – but it's enough, I think, for us." And even as he spoke I felt a rope slip slowly around my neck and tighten. "As for our other problem, since I have been here the first, then the horse is mine. Fair, no? Like your cricket?"

"Cricket! Cricket!" said the young man. "Who ever heard

of that barbarous game in Wales? That's a game for the rotten English. Rugby, that's my game, and that's not a game. That's a religion, that is — where I come from. I played before the war stopped me, and in Wales we say that a loose ball is our ball."

"Sorry?" said the German, his eyebrows furrowed with concern. "I cannot understand what you mean by this."

"Doesn't matter. Not important, not anymore. We could have settled all this peaceful like — the, the war, I mean — and I'd be back in my valley and you'd be back in yours. Still, it's not your fault, I don't suppose. Nor mine, neither, come to that."

By now the cheering from both sides had subsided and both armies looked on in total silence as the two men talked together beside me. The Welshman was stroking my nose and feeling my ears. "You know horses, then?" said the tall German. "How bad is his wounded leg? Is it broken, do you think? He seems not to walk on it."

The Welshman bent over and lifted my leg gently and expertly, wiping away the mud from around the wound. "He's a mess, all right, but I don't think it's broken. It's a bad wound, though, a deep gash — wire, by the look of it. Got to get him seen to quickly, or else the poison will set in, and then there won't be a lot anyone can do for him. Cut like that, he must have lost a lot of blood already. Question is, though, who takes him? We've got a veterinary hospital somewhere back behind our lines that could take care of him, but I expect you've got one, too."

"Yes, I think so. Somewhere it must be, but I do not know exactly where," the German said slowly. And then he dug deep in his pocket and produced a coin. "You choose the side you want, 'head or tail,' I think you say. I will show the coin to everyone on both sides and everyone will know that whichever side wins the horse it is only by chance. Then no one loses any pride, yes? And everyone will be happy."

The Welshman looked up admiringly and smiled. "All right, then, you go ahead. You show them the coin, and then you toss and I'll call."

The German held the coin up in the sun and then turned a full slow circle before spinning it high and glinting into the air. As it fell to the ground, the Welshman called out in a loud, resonant voice so that all the world could hear, "Heads!"

"Well," said the German, stooping to pick it up. "That's the face of my Kaiser looking up at me out of the mud, and he does not look pleased with me. So I am afraid you have won. The horse is yours. Take good care of him, my friend," and he picked up the rope again and handed it to the Welshman. As he did so, he held out his other hand in a gesture of friendship and reconciliation, a smile lighting his worn face. "In an hour, maybe, or two," he said, "we will be trying our best again each other to kill. God only knows why we do it, and I think He has maybe forgotten why. Good-bye, Welshman. We have shown them, haven't we? We have shown them that any problem can be solved between people if only they can trust each other. That is all it needs, no?"

The little Welshman shook his head in disbelief as he took the rope. "I think if they would let you and me have an hour or two out here together, we could sort out this whole wretched mess. There would be no more weeping widows and crying children in my valley and no more in yours. If worse came to worst, we could decide it all on the flip of a coin, couldn't we?"

"If we did," said the German with a chuckle. "If we did it that way, then it would be our turn to win. And maybe your Lloyd George would not like that." And he put his hands on the Welshman's shoulders for a moment. "Take care, my friend, and good luck. Auf Wiedersehen." And he turned away and walked slowly back across no-man's-land to the wire.

"Same to you," the Welshman shouted after him, and then he, too, turned and led me away back toward the line of khaki soldiers, who began now to laugh and cheer with delight as I limped toward them through the gap in the wire.

CHAPTER 17

IT WAS ONLY WITH THE GREATEST DIFFICULTY THAT I STAYED standing on my three good legs in the veterinary wagon that carried me that morning away from the heroic little Welshman who had brought me in. A milling crowd of soldiers surrounded me to cheer me on my way. But out on the long, rattling roads I was very soon shaken off my balance and fell in an ungainly, uncomfortable heap on the floor of the wagon. My injured leg throbbed terribly as the wagon rocked from side to side on its slow journey away from the battle front. The wagon was drawn by two stocky black horses, both well groomed and immaculate in well-oiled harnesses. Weakened by long hours of pain and starvation, I had not the strength even to get to my feet when I felt the wheels below me running at last on smooth pavement, and the wagon came to a jerking standstill in the warm, pale autumn sunshine. My arrival was greeted by a chorus of excited neighing and I raised my head to look. I could just see over the side of the wagon a wide, cobbled courtyard with magnificent stables on either side and a great house with turrets beyond. Over every stable door were the heads of inquisitive horses, ears pricked. There were men in khaki walking everywhere, and a few were running now toward me, one of them carrying a rope halter.

Unloading was painful, for I had little strength left and my legs had gone numb after the long journey. But they got me to my feet and walked me backward gently down the ramp. I found myself the center of anxious and admiring attention in the middle of the courtyard, surrounded by a cluster of soldiers who inspected minutely every part of me, feeling me all over.

"What in thunder do you think you're doing?" came a booming voice echoing across the courtyard. "It's a horse. It's a horse just like the others." A huge man was striding toward us, his boots crisp on the cobbles. His heavy red face was half hidden by the shade of his peaked cap that almost touched his nose and by an auburn mustache that spread upward from his lips to his ears. "It may be a famous horse. It may be the only thundering horse in the whole thundering war brought in alive from no-man's-land. But it is only a horse, and a dirty horse at that. I've had some rough-looking specimens brought in here in my time, but this is the scruffiest, dirtiest, muddiest horse I have ever seen. He's a thundering disgrace, and you're all standing around looking at him." He wore three broad stripes on his arm and the creases in his immaculate khaki uniform were razor sharp. "Now, there's a hundred or more sick horses here in this hospital and there's just twelve of us to look after them. This here young lazybones was detailed to look after this one when he arrived, so the rest of you guys can get back to your duties. Move it, you idle monkeys, move it!" And the men scattered in all directions, leaving me with a young soldier who began to lead me away toward a stable. "And you," came that booming voice again, "Major Martin will be down from the house in ten minutes to examine that horse. Make sure that horse is so thundering clean and thundering shiny you could use him as a shaving mirror, right?"

"Yes, Sergeant," came the reply. A reply that sent a sudden shiver of recognition through me. Quite where I had heard the voice before I did not know. I knew only that those two words sent a tremor of joy and hope and expectation through my body and warmed me from the inside out. He led me slowly across the cobbles, and I tried all the while to see his face better. But he kept just that much ahead of me so that all I could see was a neatly shaven neck and a pair of pink ears.

"How the devil did you get yourself stuck out there in no-man's-land, you old silly?" he said. "That's what everyone wants to know ever since the message came back that they'd be bringing you here. And how the devil did you get yourself in such a state? I swear there's not an inch of you that isn't covered in mud or blood. No telling what you look like under all that mess. Still, we'll soon see. I'll tie you up here and get the worst of it off in the open air. Then I'll brush you up in the right way before the officer gets here. Come on, you silly, you. Once I've got you cleaned up, then the officer can see you and he'll tidy up the nasty cut of yours. Can't give you food, I'm sorry to say, nor any water, not till he says so. That's what the sergeant told me. That's just in case they have to operate on you." And the way he whistled as he cleaned out the brushes was the whistle that went with the voice I knew. It confirmed my rising hopes, and I knew then that I could not be mistaken. In my overwhelming delight, I reared up on my back legs and cried out to him to recognize me. I wanted to make him see who I was. "Hey, careful there, you silly. Nearly knocked my hat off," he said gently, keeping a firm hold on the rope and smoothing my nose as he always had done whenever I was unhappy. "No need for that. You'll be all right. Lot of fuss about nothing. Knew a young horse once just like you, he was really proper jumpy he was till I got to know him and he got to know me."

"You talking to them horses again, Albert?" came a voice from inside the next stable. "God's truth! What makes you think they understand a word you say?"

"Some of them may not, David," said Albert. "But one day, one day one of them will. He'll come in here and he'll recognize my voice. He's bound to come in here. And then you'll see a horse that understands every word that's said to him."

"You're not going on about your Joey again?" The head that came with the voice leaned over the stable door. "Won't you ever give it up, Berty? I've told you before if I've told you a thousand times. They say there's near half a million horses out here, and you joined the Veterinary Corps just on the off chance you might come across him." I pawed the ground with my bad leg in an effort to make Albert look at me more closely, but he just patted my neck and set to work cleaning me up. "There's just one chance in half a million that your Joey walks in here. You got to be more realistic. He could be dead – a lot of them are. He could have gone off to Palestine with the cavalry. He could be anywhere along hundreds of miles of trenches. If you weren't so good with horses, and if you weren't the best friend I had, I'd think you'd gone a bit screwy the way you go on about your Joey."

"You'll understand why when you see him, David," Albert said crouching down to scrape the caked mud off my underside. "You'll see. There's no horse like him anywhere in the whole world. He's a bright red bay with a black mane and tail. He has a white cross on his forehead and four white socks that are all even to the last inch. He stands over sixteen hands and he's perfect from head to tail. I can tell you, I can tell you that when you see him you'll know him. I could pick him out of a crowd of a thousand horses. There's just something about him. Captain Nicholls, you know, he's dead now – the one I told you about that bought Joey from my father, he sent me Joey's picture – he knew it. He saw it the first time he set eyes on him. I'll find him, David. That's what I came all this way for, and I'm going to find him. Either I'll find him, or he'll find me. I told you, I made him a promise, and I'm going to keep it."

"You're crazy as a loon, Berty," said his friend opening a stable door and coming over to examine my leg. "Crazy as a loon, that's all I can say." He picked up my hoof and lifted it gently. "This one's got white socks on his front legs, anyway – that's as far as I can tell under all this blood and mud. I'll just sponge the wound away a bit, clean it up for you while I'm here. You'll never get this one cleaned up in time else. And I've finished mucking out my stables. Not a lot else to do, and it looks as if you could do with a hand. Old Sergeant Thunder won't mind, not if I've done all he told me, and I have."

The two men worked tirelessly on me, scraping and brushing and washing. I stood quite still trying only to nuzzle Albert to make him turn and look at me. But he was busy at my tail and my hindquarters now.

"Three," said his friend, washing off another of my hooves. "That's three white socks."

"Stop it, David," said Albert. "I know what you think. I know everyone thinks I'll never find him. There's thousands of army horses with four white socks – I know that, but there's only one with a blaze in the shape of a cross on the forehead. And how many horses shine red like fire in the evening sun? I tell you, there's not another one like him, not in the whole wide world."

"Four," said David. "That's four legs and four white socks. Only the cross on the forehead now, and a splash of red paint on this muddy mess of a horse, and you'll have your Joey standing here."

"Don't tease," said Albert quietly. "Don't tease, David. You know how serious I am about Joey. It'll mean all the world to me to find him again. Only friend I ever had before I came to the war. I told you. I grew up with him, I did. Only creature on this earth I felt any kinship for."

David was standing now by my head. He lifted my mane and brushed gently at first then vigorously at my forehead, blowing the dust away from my eyes. He peered closely and then set to again brushing down toward the end of my nose and up again between my ears till I tossed my head with impatience.

"Berty," he said quietly. "I'm not teasing, honest I'm not. Not now. You said your Joey had four white socks, all even to the inch? Right?"

"Right," said Albert, still brushing away at my tail.

"And you said Joey had a white cross on his forehead?"

"Right." Albert was still completely disinterested.

"Now, I have never even seen a horse like that, Berty," said David, using his hand to smooth down the hair on my forehead. "Wouldn't have thought it possible."

"Well, it is, I tell you," said Albert sharply. "And he was red, flaming red in the sunlight, like I said."

"I wouldn't have thought it possible," his friend went on, keeping his voice in check. "Not until now, that is."

"Oh, can it, David," Albert said, and there was a genuine irritation in his voice now. "I've told you, haven't I? I told you I'm serious about Joey."

"So am I, Berty. Dead serious. No messing. I'm serious. This horse has four white socks – all evenly marked like you said. This horse has a clear white cross on his forehead. This horse, as you can see for yourself, has a black mane and tail. This horse stands over sixteen hands, and when he's cleaned up, he'll look pretty as a picture. And this horse is a red bay under all that mud, just like you said, Berty."

As David was speaking, Albert suddenly dropped my tail and moved slowly around me running his hand along my back. Then at last we stood facing each other. There was a rougher hue to his face, I thought; he had more lines around his eyes and he was a broader, bigger man in his uniform than I remembered him. But he was my Albert, and there was no doubt about it, he was my Albert.

"Joey?" he said tentatively, looking into my eyes. "Joey?" I tossed up my head and called out to him in my happiness, so that the sound echoed around the yard and brought horses and men to the door of their stables. "It could be," said Albert quietly. "You're right, David – it could be him. It sounds like him even. But there's one way I know for sure," and he untied my rope and pulled the halter off my head. Then he turned and walked away to the gateway before facing me, cupping his hands to his lips and whistling. It was his owl whistle, the same low, stuttering whistle he had used to call me when we were walking out together back at home on the farm all those long years before. Suddenly there was no longer any pain in my leg and I trotted easily over toward him and buried my nose in his shoulder. "It's him, David," Albert said, putting his arms around my neck and hanging on to my mane. "It's my Joey. I've found him. He's come back to me just like I said he would."

"See?" said David wryly. "What did I tell you? See? Not often wrong, am I?"

"Not often," Albert said. "Not often, and not this time."

CHAPTER 18

I N THE EUPHORIC DAYS THAT FOLLOWED OUR REUNION, THE nightmare I had lived through seemed to fade into unreality, and the war itself was suddenly a million miles away and of no consequence. At last there were no guns to be heard, and the only vivid reminder that suffering and conflict was still going on were the regular arrivals of the veterinary wagons from the front.

Major Martin cleaned my wound and stitched it up, and though at first I could still put little weight on it, I felt in myself stronger with every day that passed. Albert was with me again, and that in itself was medicine enough; but properly fed once more with warm mash each morning and a never-ending supply of sweet-scented hay, my recovery seemed only a matter of time. Albert, like the other veterinary orderlies, had many other horses to care for, but he would spend every spare minute he could find fussing over me in the stable. To the other soldiers I was something of a celebrity, so I was scarcely ever left alone in my stable. There always seemed to be one or two faces looking admiringly over my door. Even old Thunder, as they called the sergeant, would inspect me overzealously, and when the others were not around he would fondle my ears and tickle me under my throat saying, "Quite a boy, aren't you? Thundering fine horse if ever I saw one. You get better now, d'you hear?"

But time passed and I did not get better. One morning I found myself quite unable to finish my mash, and every sharp sound, like the kick of a bucket or the rattle of the bolt on the stable door, seemed to set me on edge and made me suddenly tense from head to tail. My forelegs, in particular, would not work as they should. They were still and tired, and I felt a great weight of pain all along my spine, creeping into my neck and even my face.

Albert noticed something was wrong when he saw the mash I had left in my bucket. "What's the matter with you, Joey?" he said anxiously, and he reached out his hand to stroke me in the way he often did when he was concerned. Even the sight of his hand coming toward me, normally a welcome sign of affection, struck an alarm in me, and I backed away from him into the corner of the stable. As

I did so, I found that the stiffness in my front legs would hardly allow me to move. I stumbled backward, falling against the brick wall at the back of the stable, and leaning there heavily. "I thought something was wrong yesterday," said Albert, standing still now in the middle of the stable. "Thought you were a little out of sorts then. Your back's as stiff as a board, and you're covered in sweat. What the devil have you been up to, you old silly?" He moved slowly now toward me and although his touch still sent an irrational tremor of fear through me, I stood my ground and allowed him to stroke me. "Maybe it was something you picked up on your travels. Maybe you ate something poisonous, is that it? But then that would have shown itself before now, surely? You'll be fine, Joey, but I'll go and fetch Major Martin just in case. He'll look you over and if there's anything wrong he'll put you right 'quick as a wink,' as my father used to say. Wonder what he would think now if he could see us together? He never believed I'd find you, either – said I was a fool to go. Said it was a fool's errand and that I'd likely get myself killed in the process. But he was a different man, Joey, after you left. He knew he'd done wrong and that seemed to take all the nastiness out of him. He seemed to live only to make up for what he'd done. He stopped his Tuesday drinking sessions, looked after Mother as he used to do when I was little, and he even began to treat me right – didn't treat me like a workhorse anymore."

I knew from the soft tone of his voice that he was trying to calm me, as he had done all those long years ago when I was a wild and frightened colt. Then his words had soothed me, but now I could not stop myself from trembling. Every nerve in my body seemed to be tense, and I was breathing heavily. Every fiber of me was consumed by a totally inexplicable sense of fear and dread. "I'll be back in a minute, Joey," he said. "Don't you worry. You'll be all right. Major Martin will fix you – he's a miracle with horses, that man is." And he backed away from me and went out.

It was not long before he was back again with his friend David, Major Martin, and Sergeant Thunder, but only Major Martin came inside the stable to examine me. The others leaned over the stable door and watched. He approached me cautiously, crouching down by my foreleg to examine my wound. Then he ran his hands all over me from my ears, down my back to my tail, before standing back to survey me from the other side of the stable. He was shaking his head ruefully as he turned to speak to the others.

"What do you think, Sergeant?" he asked.

"Same as you, from the look of him, sir," said Sergeant Thunder. "He's standing there like a block of wood, tail stuck out, can hardly move his head. Not much doubt about it, is there, sir?"

"None," said Major Martin. "None whatsoever. We've had a lot of it out here. If it isn't confounded rusty barbed wire, then it's shrapnel wounds. One little fragment left inside, one cut – that's all it takes. I've seen it time and again. I'm sorry, my boy," the major said, putting his hand on Albert's shoulder to console him. "I know how much this horse means to you. But there's precious little we can do for him, not in his condition."

"What do you mean, sir?" Albert asked, a tremor in his voice. "How do you mean, sir? What's the matter with him, sir? Can't be a lot wrong, can there? He was right as rain yesterday, except he wasn't finishing his feed. Little stiff, maybe, but otherwise right as rain he was."

"It's tetanus, son," said Sergeant Thunder. "Lockjaw they call it. It's written all over him. That wound of his must have festered before we got him here. And once a horse has tetanus, there's very little chance, very little indeed."

"Best to end it quickly," Major Martin said. "No point in an animal suffering. Better for him and better for you."

"No, sir," Albert protested, still incredulous. "No you can't, sir. Not with Joey. We must try something. There must be something you can do. You can't just give up, sir. You can't. Not with Joey."

David spoke up now in support. "Begging your pardon, sir," he said. "But I remember you telling us when we first came here that a horse's life is maybe even more important than a man's, 'cause a horse hasn't got no evil in him except any that's put there by men. I remember you saying that our job in the veterinary corps was to work night and day, twenty-six hours a day if need be to save and help every horse that we could, that every horse was valuable in himself and valuable to the war effort. No horse, no guns. No horse, no ammunition. No horse, no cavalry. No horse, no ambulances. No horse, no water for the troops at the front. Lifeline of the whole army, you said, sir. We must never give up, you said, 'cause where there's life there's still hope. That's what you said, sir, begging your pardon, sir."

"You watch your lip, son," said Sergeant Thunder sharply. "That's no way to speak to an officer. If the major here thought there was a chance in a million of savin' this poor animal, he'd have a crack at it, wouldn't you, sir? Isn't that right, sir?"

Major Martin looked hard at Sergeant Thunder, taking his meaning, and then nodded slowly. "All right, Sergeant. You made your point. Of course there's a chance," he said carefully. "But if once we start with a case of tetanus, then it's a full-time job for one man for a month or more, and even then the horse has hardly more than one chance in a thousand, if that."

"Please, sir," Albert pleaded. "Please, sir. I'll do it all, sir, and I'll fit in my other horses, too, sir. Honest I will, sir."

"And I'll help him, sir," David said. "All the guys will. I know they will. You see, sir, that Joey's special for everyone here, what with his being Berty's own horse back home and all."

"That's the spirit, son," said Sergeant Thunder. "And it's true, sir, there is something special about this one, you know, after all he's been through. With your permission, sir, I think we ought to give him that chance. You have my personal guarantee, sir, that no other horse will be neglected. Stables will be run shipshape, like always."

Major Martin put his hands on the stable door. "Right, Sergeant," he said. "You're on. I like a challenge as well as the next man. I want a sling rigged up in here. This horse must not be allowed to get off his legs. Once he's down, he'll never get up again. I want a note added to standing orders, Sergeant, that no one's to talk in anything but a whisper in this yard. He won't like any noise, not with tetanus. I want a bed of short, clean straw — and fresh every day. I want the windows covered over so that he's always kept in the dark. He's not to be fed any hay — he could choke on it — just milk and oatmeal gruel. And it's going to get worse before it gets better — if it does. You'll find his mouth will lock tighter as the days go by, but he must go on feeding and he must drink. If he doesn't, then he'll die. I want a twenty-four-hour watch on this horse — that means a man posted in here all day and every day. Clear?"

"Yes, sir," said Sergeant Thunder, smiling broadly under his mustache. "And if I may say so, sir, I think you've made a very wise decision. I'll see to it, sir. Now, look lively, you two. You heard what the officer said."

That same day a sling was strung up around me and my weight supported from the beams above. Major Martin opened up my wound again, cleaned and cauterized it. He returned every few hours after that to examine me. It was Albert, of course, who stayed with me most of the time, holding up the bucket to my mouth so that I could suck in the warm milk or gruel. At nights, David and he slept side by side in the corner of the stable, taking turns to watch me.

As I had come to expect, and as I needed, Albert talked to me all he could to comfort me, until sheer fatigue drove him back into his corner to sleep. He talked much of his father and mother and about the farm. He talked of a girl he had been seeing up in the village for the few months before he left for France. She didn't know anything about horses, he said, but that was her only fault.

The days passed slowly and painfully for me. The stiffness in my front legs spread to my back and intensified; my appetite was becoming more limited each day, and I could scarcely summon the energy or enthusiasm to suck in the food I knew I needed to stay alive. In the darkest days of my illness, when I felt sure each day might be my last, only Albert's constant presence kept alive in me the will to live. His devotion, his unwavering faith that I would indeed recover, gave me the heart to go on. All around me I had friends. David and all the veterinary orderlies, Sergeant Thunder and Major Martin – they were all a source of great encouragement to me. I knew how desperately they were willing me to live, although I often wondered whether they wanted it for me or for Albert, because I knew they held him in such high esteem. But on reflection, I think perhaps they cared for both of us as if we were their brothers.

Then, one winter's night after long painful weeks in the sling, I felt a sudden looseness in my throat and neck, so much so that I could call out, albeit softly, for the first time. Albert was sitting in the corner of the stable as usual with his back against the wall, his knees drawn up and his elbows resting on his knees. His eyes were closed, so I nickered again softly, but it was loud enough to wake him. "Was that you, Joey?" he asked, pulling himself to his feet. "Was that you, you old silly? Do it again, Joey. I might have been dreaming. Do it again." So I did and in so doing I lifted my head for the first time in weeks and shook it. David heard it, too, and was on his feet and shouting over the stable door for everyone to come. Within minutes the stable was full of excited soldiers. Sergeant Thunder pushed his way through and stood before me. "Standing orders say whisper," he said. "And that was no thundering whisper I heard. What's up? What's all the hullabaloo?"

"He moved, Sarge," Albert said. "His head moved easily and he neighed."

"'Course he did, son," said Sergeant Thunder. "'Course he did. He's going to make it. Like I said he would. I always told you he would, didn't I? And have any of you lazy-bones ever known me to be wrong? Well, have you?"

"Never, Sarge," said Albert, grinning from ear to ear. "He

is getting better, isn't he, Sarge? I'm not just imagining it, am I?"

"No, son," said Sergeant Thunder. "Your Joey is going to be all right by the looks of him, long as we keep him quiet and so long as we don't rush him. I just hope that if I'm ever sick, I have nurses around me that look after me like you boys have this horse. One thing, though: looking at you, I'd like them to be a whole lot prettier!"

Shortly after, I could use my legs again and then the stiffness left my back forever. They took me out of the sling and walked me one spring morning out into the sunshine of the paved yard. It was a triumphant parade, with Albert leading me, carefully walking backward and talking to me all the while. "You've done it, Joey. You've done it. Everyone says the war's going to be over soon — I know we've been saying that for a long time, but I feel it in my bones this time. It'll be finished before long, and then we'll both be going home, back to the farm. I can't wait to see the look on Father's face when I bring you back up the road. I just can't wait."

CHAPTER 19

B UT THE WAR DID NOT END. INSTEAD, IT SEEMED TO MOVE ever closer to us, and we heard once again the ominous rumble of gunfire. My convalescence was almost over now, and though still weak from my illness, I was already being used for light work around the veterinary hospital. I worked in a team of two, hauling hay and feed from the nearest station or pulling the manure cart around the yard. I felt fresh and eager for work once more. My legs and shoulders filled out and as the weeks passed I found I was able to work longer hours in the harness. Sergeant Thunder had detailed Albert to be with me whenever I was working so that we were scarcely ever apart. But from time to time, Albert, like all the veterinary orderlies, would be dispatched to the front with the veterinary wagon to bring back the latest horse casualties, and then I would pine and fret, my head over the stable door, until I heard the echoing rumble of the wheels on the cobbles and saw his cheery wave as he came in under the archway and into the yard.

In time I, too, went back to the war, back to the front line, back to the whine and roar of the shells that I had hoped I had left behind me forever. Fully recovered now and the pride of Major Martin and his veterinary unit, I was often used as the lead horse in the tandem team that hauled the veterinary wagon back and forth to the front. But Albert was always with me, and so I was never afraid of the guns anymore. Like Topthorn before him, he seemed to sense that I needed a continual reminder that he was with me and protecting me. His soft gentle voice, his songs, and his whistling tunes held me steady as the shells came down.

All the way there and back he would be talking to me to reassure me. Sometimes it would be of the war. "David says the Germans are about finished," he said, humming, one summer's day as we passed line upon line of infantry and cavalry going up to the front line. We were carrying an exhausted gray mare, a water-carrier that had been rescued from the mud at the front. "Almost knocked us out, they did, farther up the line, they say. But David says that that was their last gasp, that once those Yankees find their fighting legs, and if we stand firm, then it could all be over by Christmas. I hope he's right, Joey. He usually is. Got a lot of respect for what David says – everyone has."

And sometimes he would talk of home and of his girl up in the village. "Maisie Brown she's called, Joey. Works in the milking parlor up Anstey's farm. And she bakes bread. Oh, Joey, she bakes bread like you've never tasted before, and even Mother says her pastries are the tastiest in the parish. Father says she's too good for me, but he doesn't mean it. He says it to please me. And she's got eyes, eyes as blue as cornflowers, hair as gold as ripe corn, and her skin smells like honeysuckle – except when she first comes out of the dairy. I keep away from her then. I've told her all about you, Joey. And she was the only one, the only one, that said I was right to come over here and find you. She didn't want me to go. Don't think that. Cried her heart out at the station when I left, so she must love me a little, right? Come on, you silly, you, say something. That's the only thing I've got against you, Joey, you're the best listener I've ever known, but I never know what the devil you're thinking. You just blink your eyes and wiggle those ears of yours from east to west and south to north. I wish you could talk, Joey. I really do."

Then, one evening there was terrible news from the

front, news that Albert's friend, David, had been killed, along with the two horses that were hauling the veterinary wagon that day. "A stray shell," Albert told me as he brought in the straw for my stable. "That's what they said it was – one stray shell out of nowhere and he's gone. I will miss him, Joey. We will both miss him, won't we?" And he sat down in the straw in the corner of the stable. "You know what he was, Joey, before the war? He had a fruit cart in London, outside Covent Garden. Thought the world of you, Joey. Told me so often enough. And he looked after me, Joey. Like a brother he was to me. Twenty years old. He had his whole life ahead of him. All wasted now 'cause of one stray shell. He always told me, Joey. He'd say, 'At least if I go, there'll be no one that'll miss me. Only my cart – and I can't take that with me, and that's a pity.' He was proud of his cart, showed me a photo of himself standing by it. All painted it was and piled high with fruit, and he was standing there with a smile like a banana spread all across his face." He looked up at me and brushed the tears from his cheeks. He spoke now through gritted teeth. "There's just you and me left now, Joey, and I tell you we're going to get home, both of us. I'm going to ring that tenor bell again in the church, I'm going to eat my Maisie's bread and pastries, and I'm going to ride you down by the river again. David always said he was somehow sure that I'd get home, and he was right. I'm going to make him right."

When the end of the war did come, it came swiftly, almost unexpectedly, it seemed, to the men around me. There was little joy, little celebration of victory, only a sense of profound relief that at last it was finished and done with. Albert left the happy cluster of men gathered together in the yard that cold November morning and strolled over to talk to me. 'Five minutes' time and it'll be finished, Joey, all over. The Germans have had about enough of it, and so have we. No one really wants to go on anymore. At eleven o'clock the guns will stop, and then that will be that. Only wish that David could have been here to see it."

Since David's death, Albert had not been himself. I had not once seen him smile or joke, and he often fell into prolonged brooding silences when he was with me. There was no more singing, no more whistling. I tried all that I could to comfort him, resting my head on his shoulder and nickering gently to him, but he seemed quite inconsolable. Even the news that the war was finally ending brought no light back to his eyes. The bell in the clock tower over the gateway rang out eleven times, and the men shook one another solemnly by the hand or clapped each other on the back before returning to the stables.

The fruits of victory were to prove bitter indeed for me, but to begin with, the end of the war changed little. The veterinary hospital operated as it always had done, and the flow of sick and injured horses seemed rather to increase than to diminish. From the yard gate we saw the unending columns of fighting men marching jauntily back to the railway stations, and we looked on as the tanks and guns and wagons rolled by on their way home. But we were left where we were. Like the other men, Albert was becoming impatient. Like them, he wanted only to get back home as quickly as possible.

The morning parade took place as usual every morning in the center of the cobbled yard, followed by Major Martin's inspection of the horses and stables. But one dreary, drizzling morning, with the wet cobbles shining gray in the early morning light, Major Martin did not inspect the stables as usual. Sergeant Thunder stood the men at ease and Major Martin announced the re-embarkment plans for the unit. He was finishing his short speech: "So we shall be at Victoria Station by six o'clock on Saturday evening – with any luck. Chances are, you'll all be home by Christmas."

"Permission to speak, sir?" Sergeant Thunder ventured.

"Carry on, Sergeant."

"It's about the horses, sir," Sergeant Thunder said. "I think the men would like to know what's going to happen with the horses. Will they be with us on the same ship, sir? Or will they be coming along later?"

Major Martin shifted his feet and looked down at his boots. He spoke softly as if he did not want to be heard. "No, Sergeant," he said. "I'm afraid the horses won't be coming with us at all." There was an audible muttering of protest from the parading soldiers.

"You mean, sir," said the Sergeant. "You mean that they'll be coming on a later ship?"

"No, Sergeant," said the Major, slapping his side with his stick, "I don't mean that. I mean exactly what I said. I mean they will not be coming with us at all. The horses will be staying in France."

"Here, sir?" said the sergeant. "But how can they, sir? Who'll be looking after them? We've got cases here that need attention all day and every day."

The major nodded, his eyes still looking at the ground. "You're not going to like what I have to tell you," he said. "I'm afraid a decision has been made to sell off many of the army's horses here in France. All the horses we have here are either sick or have been sick. It's not considered worth-while to transport them back home. My orders are to hold a horse sale here in this courtyard tomorrow morning. A notice has been posted in neighboring towns to that effect. They are to be sold by auction."

"Auctioned off, sir? Our horses to be put under the hammer, after all they've been through?" The sergeant spoke politely, but only just. "But you know what that means, sir? You know what will happen?"

"Yes, Sergeant," said Major Martin. "I know what will happen to them. But there's nothing anyone can do. We're in the army, Sergeant, and I don't have to remind you that orders are orders."

"But you know what they'll go for," said Sergeant Thunder, barely disguising the disgust in his voice. "There's thousands of our horses out here in France, sir. War veterans they are. D'you mean to say that after all they've been through, after all we've done looking after them, after all you've done, sir — that they're to end up like that? I can't believe they mean it, sir."

"Well, I'm afraid they do," said the major stiffly. "Some of them may end up as you suggest — I can't deny it, Sergeant. You've every right to be indignant, every right. I'm not too happy about it myself, as you can imagine. But by tomorrow, most of these horses will have been sold off, and we shall be moving out ourselves the day after. And you know, Sergeant, and I know, there's not a blessed thing I can do about it."

Albert's voice rang out across the yard. "What, all of them, sir? Every one of them? Even Joey that we brought back from the dead? Even him?"

Major Martin said nothing, but turned on his heel and walked away.

CHAPTER 20

THERE WAS AN AIR OF DETERMINED CONSPIRACY IN THE yard that day. Whispering groups of men in dripping overcoats, their collars turned up to keep the rain from their necks, huddled together, their voices low and earnest. Albert seemed scarcely to notice me all day. He would neither talk to me nor even look at me, but hurried through the daily routine of mucking out, haying up, and grooming in a deep and gloomy silence. I knew, as every horse in the yard knew, that we were threatened. I was torn with anxiety.

An ominous shadow had fallen on the yard that morning, and not one of us could settle in our stables. When we were led out for exercise, we were jumpy and skittish, and Albert, like the other soldiers, responded with impatience, jerking sharply at my halter, something I had never known him to do before.

That evening, the men were still talking, but now Sergeant Thunder was with them and they all stood together in the darkening yard. I could just see in the last of the evening light the glint of money in their hands. Sergeant Thunder carried a small tin box that was being passed around from one to the other and I heard the clink of coins as they were dropped in. The rain had stopped now, and it was a still evening, so that I could just make out Sergeant Thunder's low, growling voice. "That's the best we can do, boys," he was saying. "It's not a lot, but then we haven't got a lot, have we? No one ever gets rich in this man's army. I'll do the bidding, like I said — it's against orders, but I'll do it. Mind you, I'm not promising anything." He paused and looked over his shoulder before going on. "I'm not supposed to tell you this — the major said not to — and make no mistake, I'm not in the habit of disobeying officers' orders. But we aren't at war anymore, and anyway, this order was more like advice, so to speak. So I'm telling you this 'cause I wouldn't like you to think badly of the major. He knows what's going on right enough. Matter of fact, the whole thing was his own idea. It was him that told me to suggest it to you in the first place. What's more, boys, he's given us every penny of his pay that he had saved up — every penny. It's not much, but it'll help. 'Course

I don't have to tell you that no one says a word about this – not one word. If this was to get about, then he gets the boot, like all of us would. So mum's the word, clear?"

"Have you got enough, Sarge?" I could hear that it was Albert's voice speaking.

"I'm hoping so, son," Sergeant Thunder said, shaking the box. "I'm hoping so. Now let's all of us get some shut-eye. I want you lazybones up bright and early in the morning and them horses looking their thundering best. It's the last thing we'll be doing for them – least we can do for them, seems to me."

And so the group dispersed, the men walking away in twos and threes, shoulders hunched against the cold, their hands deep in their overcoat pockets. One man only was left standing by himself in the yard. He stood for a moment looking up at the sky before walking over toward my stable. I could tell it was Albert from the way he walked – it was that rolling farmer's gait with the knees never quite straightening up after each stride. He pushed back his peaked cap as he leaned over the stable door. "I've done all I can, Joey," he said. "We all have. I can't tell you any more 'cause I know you'd understand every word I said, and then you'd only worry yourself sick with it. This time, Joey, I can't even make you a promise like I did when Father sold you off to the army. I can't make you a promise 'cause I don't know whether I can keep it. I asked old Thunder to help and he helped. I asked the major to help and he helped. And now I've just asked God, 'cause when all's said and done, it's all up to Him. We've done all we can, that's for certain sure. I remember old Miss Wirtle telling me once in Sunday school back home: 'God helps those that helps themselves.' Mean old devil she was, but she knew her scriptures well enough. God bless you, Joey. Sleep tight." And he put out his clenched fist and rubbed my muzzle, and then stroked each of my ears in turn before leaving me alone in the dark of the stables. It was the first time he had talked to me like that since the day David had been reported killed, and it warmed my heart just to listen to him.

The day dawned bright over the clock tower, throwing the long, lean shadows of the poplars beyond across the cobbles that glistened with frost. Albert was up with the others before reveille was blown, so that by the time the first buyers arrived in the yard in their carts and cars, I was fed and watered and groomed so hard that my winter coat gleamed red as I was led out into the morning sun.

The buyers were gathered in the middle of the yard, and we were led, all those that could walk, around the perimeter of the yard in a grand parade, before being brought out one by one to face the auctioneer and the buyers. I found myself waiting in my stable watching every horse in the yard being sold ahead of me. I was, it seemed, to be the last to be brought out. Distant echoes of an earlier auction sent me suddenly into a feverish sweat, but I forced myself to remember Albert's reassuring words of the night before, and in time my heart stopped racing. So when Albert led me out into the yard, I was calm and easy in my stride. I had unswerving faith in him as he patted my neck gently and whispered secretly in my ear. There were audible and visible signs of approval from the buyers as he walked me around in a tight circle, bringing me at last to a standstill facing a line of red, craggy faces and grasping, greedy eyes. Then I noticed in among the shabby coats and hats of the buyers, the still, tall figure of Sergeant Thunder towering above them, and to one side the entire veterinary unit lined up along the wall and watching the proceedings anxiously. The bidding began.

I was clearly much in demand, for the bidding was swift to start with, but as the price rose, I could see more heads shaking, and very soon there seemed to be only two bidders left. One was old Thunder himself, who would touch the corner of his cap with his stick, almost like a salute, to make his bid, and the other was a thin, wiry little man with weasel eyes who wore on his face a smile so full of consummate greed and evil that I could hardly bear to look at him. Still the price moved up. "At twenty-five, twenty-six. At twenty-seven. Twenty-seven I'm bid. On my right. Twenty-seven I'm bid. Any more, please? It's against the sergeant there, at twenty-seven. Any more, please. He's a fine young animal, as you see. Got to be worth a lot more than this. Any more, please?" But the sergeant was shaking his head now, his eyes looked down and acknowledged defeat.

"Oh God, no," I heard Albert whisper beside me. "Dear God, not him. He's one of them, Joey. He's been buying all morning. Old Thunder says he's the butcher from Cambrai. Please, God, no."

"Well, then, if there are no more bids, I'm selling to Monsieur Cirac of Cambrai at twenty-seven English pounds. Is that all? Selling then for twenty-seven. Going, going . . ."

"Twenty-eight," came a voice from among the buyers, and I saw a white-haired old man leaning heavily on his stick, shuffle slowly forward through the buyers until he stood in front of them. "I'm bidding twenty-eight of your English pounds," said the old man, speaking in hesitant English. "And I'll bid for so long and so high as I need to, I advise you, sir," he said, turning to the butcher from Cambrai.

"I advise you not to try to outbid me. For this horse I will pay one hundred English pounds if I must do. No one will have this horse except me. This is my Emilie's horse. It is hers by right." Before he spoke her name I had not been quite sure that my eyes and ears were not deceiving me, for the old man had aged many years since I had last set eyes on him, and his voice was thinner and weaker than I remembered. But now I was sure. This was indeed Emilie's grandfather standing before me, his mouth set with grim determination, his eyes glaring around him, challenging anyone to try to outbid him. No one said a word. The butcher from Cambrai shook his head and turned away. Even the auctioneer had been stunned into silence, and there was some delay before he brought his hammer down on the table and I was sold.

CHAPTER 21

THERE WAS A LOOK OF RESIGNED DEJECTION ON SERGEANT Thunder's face as he and Major Martin spoke together with Emilie's grandfather after the sale. The yard was empty now of horses, and the buyers were all driving away. Albert and his friends stood around me commiserating with one another, all of them trying to comfort Albert. "No need to worry, Albert," one of them was saying. "After all, could have been worse, couldn't it? I mean, a lot more'n half of our horses have gone to the butchers and that's definite. At least we know Joey's safe enough with that old farmer man."

"How do you know that?" Albert asked. "How do you know he's a farmer?"

"I heard him telling old Thunder, didn't I? Heard him saying he's got a farm down in the valley. Told old Thunder that Joey would never have to work again so long as he lived. Kept yammering on about a girl called Emilie or something. Couldn't understand half of what he was saying."

"Dunno what to make of him," said Albert. "Sounds mad as a hatter, the way he goes on. 'Emilie's horse by right' – whoever she may be. Isn't that what the old man said? What the devil did he mean by that? If Joey belongs to anyone by right, then he belongs to the army, and if he doesn't belong to the army, he belongs to me."

"Better ask him yourself, Albert," said someone else. "Here's your chance. He's coming over this way with the major and old Thunder."

Albert stood with his arm under my chin, his hand reaching up to scratch me behind my ear, just where he knew I liked it best. As the Major came closer, though, he took his hand away, came to attention, and saluted smartly. "Begging your pardon, sir," he said. "I'd like to thank you for what you did, sir. I know what you did, sir, and I'm grateful. Not your fault we didn't quite make it, but thanks all the same, sir."

"I don't know what he's talking about," said Major Martin. "Do you, Sergeant?"

"Can't imagine, sir," said Sergeant Thunder. "They get like that, you know, sir, these farmboys. It's 'cause they're raised on cider instead of milk. It's true, sir – goes to their heads, sir. Must be true, right?"

"Begging your pardon, sir," Albert went on, puzzled by their levity. "I'd like to ask the Frenchman, sir, since he's gone and bought my Joey. I'd like to ask him about what he said, sir, about this Emilie, or whatever she was called."

"It's a long story," said Major Martin, and he turned to the old man. "Maybe you would like to tell him yourself, monsieur? This is the young man we were speaking of, monsieur, the one who grew up with the horse and who came all the way to France just to look for him."

Emilie's grandfather stood looking sternly up at my Albert from under his bushy white eyebrows, and then his face cracked suddenly and he held out his hand and smiled. Although surprised, Albert reached and shook his hand. "So, young man. We have much in common you and I. I am French and you are Tommy. True, I am old and you are young. But we share a love for this horse, do we not? And I am told by the officer here that at home in England you are a farmer, like I am. It is the best thing to be, and I say that with the wisdom of years behind me. What do you keep on your farm?"

"Sheep, sir, mostly. A few beef cattle and some pigs," said Albert. "Plow a few fields of barley as well."

"So, it was you that trained the horse to be a farm horse?" said the old man. "You did well, my son, very well. I can see the question in your eyes before you ask it, so I'll tell you how I know. You see, your horse and I are old friends. He came to live with us – oh, it was a long time ago now, not long after the war began. He was captured by the Germans and they used him for pulling their ambulance cart from the hospital to the front line and back again. There was with him another wonderful horse, a big shining black horse, and the two of them came to live in our farm that was near the German field hospital. My little granddaughter, Emilie, cared for them and came to love them like her own family. I was all the family she had left – the war had taken the rest. The horses lived with us for maybe a year, maybe less, maybe more – it does not matter. The Germans were kind and gave us the horses when they left, and so they became ours, Emilie's and mine. Then, one day they came back, different Germans, not kind like the others; they needed horses for their guns, and so they took our horses away with them when they left. There was nothing I could do. After that, my Emilie lost the will to live. She was a sick child, anyway, but now with her family dead and her new family taken from her, she no longer had anything to live for. She just faded away and died last year. She was only fifteen years old. But before she died, she made me promise her that I would find the horses somehow and look after them. I have been to many horse sales, but I have never found the other one, the black one. But now at last I have found one of them to take home and care for as I promised my Emilie."

He leaned more heavily on his stick now with both hands. He spoke slowly, choosing his words carefully. "Tommy," he went on. "You are a farmer, a British farmer and you will understand that a farmer, whether he is British or French – even a Belgian farmer – never gives things away. He can never afford to. We have to live, do we not? Your major and your sergeant have told me how much you love this horse. They told me how every one of these men tried so hard to buy this horse. I think that is a noble thing. I think my Emilie would have liked that. I think she would understand, that she would want me to do what I will do now. I am an old man. What would I do with Emilie's horse? He cannot grow fat in a field all his life, and soon I will be too old to look after him, anyway. And if I remember him well, and I do, he loves to work, does he not? I have – how you say? – a proposition to make to you. I will sell my Emilie's horse to you."

"Sell?" said Albert. "But I cannot pay you enough to buy

him. You must know that. We collected only twenty-six pounds between us and you paid twenty-eight pounds. How can I afford to buy him from you?"

"You do not understand, my friend," the old man said, suppressing a chuckle. "You do not understand at all. I will sell you this horse for one English penny, *and* for a solemn promise – that you will always love this horse as much as my Emilie did and that you will care for him until the end of his days. And more than this, I want you to tell everyone about my Emilie and about how she looked after your Joey and the big black horse when they came to live with us. You see, my friend, I want my Emilie to live on in people's hearts. I shall die soon, in a few years, no more, and then no one will remember my Emilie as she was. I have no other family left alive to remember her. She will be just a name on a gravestone that no one will read. So I want you to tell your friends at home about my Emilie. Otherwise it will be as if she had never even lived. Will you do this for me? That way she will live forever, and that is what I want. Is it a bargain between us?"

Albert said nothing, for he was too moved to speak. He simply held out his hand in acceptance, but the old man ignored it, put his hands on Albert's shoulder, and kissed him on both cheeks. "Thank you," he said. And then, he turned and shook hands with every soldier in the unit and at last hobbled back and stood in front of me. "Good-bye, my friend," he said, and he touched me lightly on my nose with his lips. "From Emilie," he said, and then walked away. He had gone only a few paces before he stopped and turned around. Wagging his knobbly stick and with a mocking, accusing grin across his face, he said, "Then it is true what we say, that there is only one thing at which the English are better than the French. They are meaner. You have not paid me my English penny, my friend." Sergeant Thunder produced a penny from the tin and gave it to Albert, who ran over to Emilie's grandfather.

"I shall treasure it," said the old man. "I shall treasure it always."

And so I came home from the war that Christmastime with my Albert riding me up into the village, and there to greet us was the silver band from the village and the rapturous pealing of the church bells. Both of us were received like conquering heroes, but we both knew that the real heroes had not come home, that they were lying out in France alongside Captain Nicholls, Topthorn, Friedrich, David, and little Emilie.

My Albert married his Maisie Brown as he said he

would. But I think she never took to me, nor I to her for that matter. Perhaps it was a feeling of mutual jealousy. I went back to my work on the land with dear old Zoey, who seemed ageless and tireless, and Albert took over the farm again and went back to ringing his tenor bell. He talked to me of many things after that, of his aging father who doted on me now almost as much as on his own grandchildren, and of the vagaries of the weather and the markets, and of course about Maisie, whose crusty bread was every bit as good as he had said. But try as I might, I never got to eat any of her pastries, and do you know, she never even offered me one.

WRITING WAR HORSE
BY MICHAEL MORPURGO

April 17, 2008, was the ninetieth anniversary of the Battle of Merkem, or the Battle of the Kippe. The Belgian army retook the hamlet of de Kippe. It was a significant advance much celebrated by the Belgians. To mark the occasion of this first Belgian victory, my grandfather Emile Cammaerts, a great poet and Belgian patriot, named my mother, who was born on April 18, 1918, Kippe. It is the name by which I've known her all my life. This is the first of many diverse influences that contributed to my writing *War Horse* many decades later.

I grew up in London just after the Second World War, a London of bomb sites and ration books. I played in bomb sites (surely the best playgrounds ever made). We had cellars for dens, crumbling walls to climb, and in amongst the rubble I made endless discoveries. An old kettle, a shoe, a penny coin, a burnt book—they all became my treasures. Only later came the growing awareness of what war had done, not just to buildings but to people's lives.

My mother often wept when she talked about the war. On the mantelpiece was a photo of my Uncle Pieter, who was shot down in 1941, two years before I was born. He looked back at me when I looked at him, and I knew he wanted to say something but couldn't. I used to talk to him sometimes, I remember. I wanted to get to know him.

A friend of the family used to come to tea sometimes. My mother always told me I must not stare at him, but I always did. I could not help myself. His face and hands were horribly scarred. I knew he had been shot down in the war and suffered dreadful burns. Here's what the war did: It burned flesh. It killed my uncle. It made my mother weep. So I grew up with the damage of war all around me. I learned that buildings you can put up again, but lives are wrecked forever.

As a schoolboy I read the great poets of the First World War—Wilfred Owen, Siegfried Sassoon, Edmund Blunden, Edward Thomas, Thomas Hardy. I learned of "the men who marched away," of "the millions of the mouthless dead," understood "the pity of war." I read Remarque's *All Quiet on the Western Front.* I saw the film. I went to see Joan Littlewood's *Oh! What a Lovely War.* Britten's great *War Requiem*—the pictures of Paul Nash and Stanley Spencer left an indelible impression on me.

In my early thirties, in 1975, we moved from Kent to Iddesleigh in Devon, where my wife Clare and I were setting up Farms for City Children, an educational charity we hoped would enrich the lives of urban children by enabling them to spend a week of their young lives living and working down on the farm.

We found ourselves living in a small, tight-knit community—Iddesleigh was a parish of less than two hundred people, a church, a post office, a village shop, a pub. Here we settled, and began our project. I had written one or two books already, but now for the first time I came across a subject that I cared about deeply, one that I felt I could write from the heart.

I was in the pub, the Duke of York. "Are you writing another book, Michael?" said the old man sitting opposite me by the fire, cradling his pint. I told him that I'd come across an old painting of a cavalry charge in the First World War. The British cavalry were charging up a hill towards the German position, one or two horses already caught up on the barbed wire. I was trying, I told him, to write the story of the First World War as seen through the eyes of a horse. "I was there in 1916," the old man told me, his eyes filling with tears. "I was there with the horses, too." He talked on for hours about the horse he'd loved and left behind at the end of the war, how the old horse had been sold off to the French butchers for meat.

I determined then and there to tell the story of such a horse. But how to tell it? I had to find a way that didn't take sides. So I conceived the notion that I might write a story of the First World War as seen through a horse's eyes, a horse that would be reared on a Devon farm, by the forebears of the village people I knew; a horse that is sold off the farm to go to the front as a British cavalry horse, is captured by the Germans and used to pull ambulances and guns, winters on a French farm. It would be the horse's-eye view of the universal suffering of that dreadful war in which ten million men died, and unknown millions of horses.

But I had yet to be convinced that I could make this work, that the horse might respond credibly, might understand the needs and anxieties of the people he came to know.

Because I had been working for so long on the farm with children, I was of course aware of the sensibilities of children towards animals, and vice versa.

It was one incident in particular that convinced me I could make my story work.

A young boy from Birmingham came to the farm with his classmates some twenty-five years ago. He was called Billy. Billy, I was told by the teachers, had been fostered by several different families, was withdrawn, and so tormented by a stammer that by the age of seven he had given up speaking at all.

One November evening, I had come to the farmhouse to read to the children. As I came into the stable yard behind the house, I found Billy standing there under the stable light, talking freely to one of the horses. He spoke confidently, knowing he was not being judged or mocked.

And I had the very strong impression that the horse was listening, and understanding, too. It was an unforgettable moment for all three of us, I think. It was that extraordinary, inspirational moment that gave me the confidence I needed to begin writing *War Horse*.

AN INTERVIEW WITH MICHAEL MORPURGO

Q: *Where do you get your inspiration from?*
A: I get my inspiration from everything that is going on around me. I travel a lot and meet people, talk to them and see new places. I also listen out for stories and things that are happening in the world and listen to the radio and read newspapers. I try to keep my eyes and ears open, and my heart, too.

Q: *How did you begin writing books for young people? Did you always want to be a writer?*
A: Not at all. I wanted to be a rugby player—my dream was to play for England. When I left school I joined the army and then was a teacher. As a teacher, I had to read the children a story every day, and my lot were bored by the book I was reading. I decided I had to do something and told them the kind of story I used to tell my kids—it was like a soap opera, and they focused on it. I could see there was magic in it for them and realized there was magic in it for me.

Q: *What was it like being the Children's Laureate, what did you have to do?*

A: I was lucky enough to be Children's Laureate from 2003 to 2005. It was an unforgettable experience. I travelled all over the country meeting people and talking to them and telling my stories. It was great to hear their stories too. One of the most valuable roles of the job of Children's Laureate was the ability to be in a position to say something about the importance of books and the love of stories. To be in a position where I could talk about these things and people would listen.

Q: *How many books have you written?*

A: Over one hundred. *Private Peaceful* was the hundredth. Sounds like a lot but that's fat ones, thin ones. All sorts.

Q: *Where do you write?*

A: On my bed where I'm most comfortable. I pile the pillows up behind me, settle back, and write by hand with my exercise book on my knees.

Q: *Are the stories true?*

A: With each one there is an element of truth. I weave different truths into the same story to make another kind of truth. So with *Kensuke's Kingdom*, there was a Japanese soldier who decided to stay behind on an island after

World War II, and people do hunt orangutans, kill the parents, and kidnap their young; and people do sail around the world on yachts, and sometimes they fall overboard....

Q: *Are your characters usually based on people you know?*
A: They aren't usually people I know as such, but perhaps a combination of different people and ideas.

Q: *What was your first book?*
A: Shan't tell you, because it wasn't much good.

Q: *What is the favorite book that you have written?*
A: *The Butterfly Lion* or *Kensuke's Kingdom* or *War Horse* or *Private Peaceful.*

Q: *How do you know when one of your ideas is good enough for a book?*
A: I get a strange sensation when I know I have hit on a good idea. It's a kind of tingling feeling all over. I often spend months weaving my story in my head, dreaming it and living it over and over again before it is ready to write down, so knowing that you have found a good idea for a story is a wonderful feeling.

Q: *What is it like knowing that millions of people have read your stories?*

A: It is a thrill to me to know that people read and hopefully enjoy my stories. I love to see the magic that well-told stories can give people—there is magic in that for me too.

Q: *What were your favorite books when you were a child?*

A: I wasn't the greatest reader when I was young and loved being read to, particularly by my mother. But the books I enjoyed reading most were adventure stories—*Treasure Island* was a favorite as was *The Jungle Book* and *The Elephant's Child* by Rudyard Kipling.

Q: *Who are your favorite authors?*

A: There are many of them. I loved the writing and storytelling of Robert Louis Stevenson, and Ted Hughes' poetry is in a class of its own.

Q: *Why do you often write about animals in your books?*

A: I think it may have something to do with the fact that animals are a good way into a story, especially for children. Animals don't judge like adults, they are accepting and will just listen. I have always been fascinated by the relationship of people and children with animals. I was a farmer for many years working on real working farms with the charity that my wife and I used to run—Farms For

City Children. My respect and love of animals grew from that.

Q: *How long does it take to write a book?*
A: It depends on how well I'm writing, how well it's flowing. But I usually spend several months dreaming it up in my head–I call it my "dreamtime," the most important part of my story inventing when I try to weave the story together, do my research, and find the right voice for the story. Once I begin writing, I write very fast and will finish a book in two or three months. Then revising it might take another month. So, on average, a novel takes upwards of six months to write.

Q: *How do you choose your illustrators?*
A: By getting to know them. I've worked for many years now with Michael Foreman. Indeed, he's suggested many stories to me, including *Farm Boy, Billy the Kid,* and *Arthur, High King of Britain.* We really do spark off each other. I've worked very well, too, with Quentin Blake, Christian Birmingham, Tony Ross, Shoo Rayner, and many others. The publishers sometimes help in choosing who should illustrate what. They know many more illustrators than I do and can visualize a book better than me. But I know what I like.

Q: *How old are you? Have you got any children? Do you have any pets?*

A: I'm very young. I'm 64 years young. I have a wife called Clare, three children, and six grandchildren. Sadly our old dog Bercelet died last year so all we have are four bantams, three hens, and a cockerel called George who loves to scratch up the flowers in the garden.

Q: *What tips would you give to young writers?*

A: The main thing is to keep your ears and eyes open all the time. To find out more about the world and have an inquisitive mind and heart.

ABOUT THE AUTHOR

MICHAEL MORPURGO IS, IN HIS OWN WORDS, "OLDISH, married with three children, and a grandfather six times over." Born in 1943, he attended schools in London, Sussex, and Canterbury (at least one of which was horrible enough to inspire him to describe it obliquely in *The Butterfly Lion*). He went on to London University to study English and French, followed by a step into the teaching profession and a job in a primary school in Kent. It was there that he discovered what he wanted to do.

In 1976, Michael and his wife Clare started the charity Farms For City Children (FFCC), which provides young children from urban areas with a week in which they work actively and purposefully on farms in the heart of the countryside. They now have three farms—Nethercott in Devon, Treginnis in Wales, and Wick in Gloucestershire. "As a teacher," Michael says, "I realized many children had little real contact with the world around them—to them the television was real. I wanted them to experience life at first hand." In the last thirty years, over 50,000 children from cities and towns throughout the United Kingdom have spent a week of their lives living and working on one of the three farms.

Living in Devon, listening to Mozart, and working with children have provided most of the stimuli Michael needs to discover and write his stories. He spends about half his life mucking out sheds with the children, feeding sheep, or milking cows; the other half he spends dreaming up and writing stories. "For me, the greater part of writing is daydreaming, dreaming the dream of my story until it hatches out—the writing down of it I always find hard. But I love finishing it, then holding the book in my hand and sharing my dream with my readers."

ALSO FROM MICHAEL MORPURGO

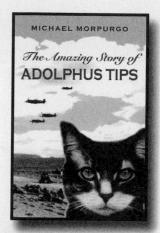

A girl's search for her missing cat gives her an up-front look at the realities of war.

A boyhood spent on the front lines of combat inspires this story set during World War I.

A boy and his dog wash up on a deserted island—and discover that they're not alone.